# The Dharma of Duluth

## By
## Konnie Ellis

Also by Konnie Ellis:
*The Ice Dancer*

"The Dharma of Duluth," by Konnie Ellis. ISBN 978-1-62137-682-8 (Softcover) 978-1-62137-707-8 (eBook.).

Library of Congress Control Number: 2015903536

Cover photo by Lane Ellis

# Dedication

In memory of my father,

Karl Egil Haldorsen

# The Dharma of Duluth

# part 1

## In the Beginning
## There Were Bears

# *one*

---

DULUTH, MINNESOTA IS THE City of Bears and Lilly is ready for another bear.

"Why not?" she says, hanging up the phone. She calls to her niece in the next room where Sarah sits in the lotus position combing her hair. Sarah saunters into the kitchen, curious at the excitement in her aunt's voice.

"What's up?"

"There's a bear up a tree in Leif Erickson Park. We need to leave right away."

Lilly is revving up the engine of the 1979 Toyota by the time Sarah gets to the driveway. She ducks down to slide into the passenger seat. The old orange car vibrates as they make the turn out of the driveway. Lilly drives down the center of the road, with both hands firmly on the steering wheel.

"Watch the road Lilly. There's a car coming up."

"Okay. They're trying to coax the bear down. You can't tranquilize it in a tree. Not if it's up too high."

Sarah was relieved when her aunt gave up the motorcycle. Still, she doesn't like her jerky driving and the sudden stops to look at flowers in someone's yard, or a cat sitting on a porch step. Once she braked to an abrupt dead stop just to tell a woman who had stepped outside to get her morning newspaper that she liked the color of her purple bathrobe. Said it was a royal color, a spiritual color. That's how Lilly met Lulu, whom they'll meet at the park. She's the source of the bear news.

Lilly pulls into the SuperOne parking lot across the street from Lake Superior and the park, happy to find her favorite parking spot available. She doesn't like congested parking lots or driving around and around to find only a small space that you have to maneuver into. They dash across London Road and cut through the rose garden toward Leif Erickson Park. Lilly slows down beside a hedge of roses, rummaging in her big yellow sunflower bag for her mini clippers so she can cut a few roses, which she insists is merely pruning, and helpful to the gardens. She stops beside a rose bush thick with coral blossoms, but Sarah talks her into waiting until after they see the bear, so they won't wilt, telling her she really shouldn't clip like that in a public garden. Lilly insists she only takes the ones that are ready to go; ones the gardener would cut that day anyway, yet she puts the clippers back in her bag.

When they reach the hilltop, Lilly starts to jog, holding her sari daintily as she dashes gracefully down the hill. Sarah lopes along beside her aunt until they find Lulu in the small crowd gathered below the treed bear near the old Viking ship. "What are they doing? I can't see," Lilly says, as she digs for her glasses. "Okay, there he is. I see him. Way up there. Ahh, poor thing."

The bear clings to the trunk of an old willow, its left back leg wedged inside the cleft of a heavy branch. He is already large, a two-year old. Lulu heard it on the radio, not long on his own and away from his mother. Lulu tells how they stay with their mothers for their first two years, learning the skills they need to survive on their own. It's in the fall when they come into town looking for food. Before hibernation. Usually they stay on the edge of town, overturning garbage cans or eating ripe apples from the trees. They hardly ever wander all the way down to the lake.

Lilly, Sarah and Lulu and the others, including a police officer who is getting instructions on his cell phone, cluster near the trunk of the tree, craning their necks looking up. The

4

officer keeps his eyes on the bear and occasionally looks over his shoulder for the guy from the zoo. The officer is a young man from Minneapolis who is unfamiliar with the ways of bears, and is much more nervous than the rest of the crowd of Duluthians.

In the park Sarah is listening to several conversations at once. A woman is telling how the bear followed Chester Creek all the way down to London Road, and a young boy who lives nearby thinks it's the bear he saw last weekend eating crab apples in Mrs. Meyer's yard.

"My knees were just plain knocking together," a woman in jeans, carrying a gardening shears, tells no one in particular. "It came right through the Mr. Lincolns and headed for the French pinks." Sarah asked if she had ever seen the movie 'Edward Scissorhands,' but she hadn't. Said she was a volunteer at the rose gardens. A distinguished old man wearing earmuffs tells the gardener to put the shears away because the bear might fall on them. Hearing his comment, everyone steps back. The bear lets out a little moan, like a sad baby.

Lilly steps up to the officer and tells him it probably won't come down until they all leave, thinking he should just tell them all to disperse, and step back out of sight himself, but before anything comes of this the zoo man arrives. They all turn to see two large men hustling across the park lawn, one in a red jacket, wearing a hat that says Happy Zoo Year, and the other in full fireman's gear.

"Everybody back. Let's get this baby down." The zoo man swaggers toward the tree, and Sarah is glad someone who seems to know what to do has arrived, as the rookie cop had made her nervous with his air of uncertainty. Backing away, she reads the back of his jacket: "Fireworks at the Duluth Zoo – Happy New Year! Happy Zoo Year!"

"They must hate that," Lilly says. "The poor animals, having to put up with fireworks when they should be sleeping. They're probably scared to death. If I weren't going to India I would organize a protest. I'll write a letter to Mayor Ness before I go," she says, looking from Sarah to Lulu as they back up the hill away from the tree.

Sarah remembers how she liked the bear houses made of stone at the zoo with their sharp angles and cubist shapes and how the bears would amble out of their caves and dive into the moat. They seemed proud, and oblivious of human spectators. Her dad had told her how the bear house was a WPA project, with a design well ahead of its time.

They find a spot half way up the hill and Lilly takes three supermarket bags from her purse for protection from the dew, and they settle down on the grass.

"It's like a play," Lulu says, chuckling to herself. Most of the crowd has gone, though a few people have parked themselves on the benches at the top of the hill.

"I can't believe I'm actually here," Lulu goes on. "This is wonderful."

Lilly agrees, it is like a play. Sara leans back on her elbows.

"Such a view, the bear in the tree, the park, Lake Superior. I just feel so lucky. It's a good day for bears," Lulu says, stretching her legs out straight. "A good day for us anyway, maybe not so good for the bear," she reconsiders.

Lulu's favorite story is about the time the mountain goat escaped from the zoo and she heard the entire chase and capture back when she had a scanner. Lilly has heard many times how the patrolman kept calling for help while sitting on the goat, which he had finally tracked down at the top of Enger Tower hill. Lulu had been as relieved as the patrolman who was sitting on the goat, when help arrived and they could finally get the goat back to the zoo.

Sarah shudders, horrified that an animal could escape from the zoo. As a child, she had nightmares about the lion getting out of the Duluth Zoo and stalking her on her way home from school.

"Shhh," Lilly shushes them. "He's singing. One of them is."

Coming from below the tree, in a clear baritone, they hear "What'll I do, when you – are far a-way – and I am all alone." Lilly hums along. "It's the zoo man. He's singing to the bear. Calming it down." They all lean forward to see what will happen. The zoo man shoos the rookie and the fireman away. They walk backwards and step behind a bush. Zoo man continues singing, though more quietly now, and slower. A rifle is visible at his side. The bear has come down a good foot.

Zoo man joins the others behind the bush and keeps humming. The bear stretches its neck and looks around the park. He looks down below the tree, and appears ready to move. Yes, the bear is coming down. He struggles to release his back foot and kicks it free out into the air, then slides down the tree so fast that Sarah leaps to her feet, ready to run. Lilly and Lulu rise, arm in arm.

As soon as the bear touches the ground, zoo man steps out and shoots the tranquilizer gun. A hit. The bear runs forward, and Lulu, Lilly and Sarah are half poised to scoot up the hill but remain standing, glued to the scene in front of them. The bear staggers, takes a few fast steps toward the bush, stands still and wobbles, then falls over onto its side, out cold. For a moment, time seems to freeze over the bear as though an unseen photographer just clicked the shutter of a big old-fashioned black box of a camera, capturing forever the scene of the fallen black bear on the green grassy slope of Leif Erickson Park beside Lake Superior. A black bear on the grass, sinking, dying, receding, deep into the primitive past of the onlookers. Three seagulls fly overhead, squawking their way out over the lake at the same time a noisy truck rumbles down the hill, bringing the scene and the people back into ordinary time.

The truck bounces down the hill and stops within yards of the bear, and a man in gray sweats steps out carrying a black bag. He walks calmly but briskly to the bear and squats down beside its head. After resting a hand on the bear's side, he strokes the bear's fur and beckons to the truck driver. The driver backs the truck up to within a few feet of the bear. He spreads a large yellow tarp next to the bear and the four men hoist the heavy, limp bear onto the tarp. Sarah remembers when her dog died, how its head was limp like that. They pull the bear along on the tarp and up into the truck where they slide him into a cage. The sound of the lock clicking shut is audible across the grounds of Leif Erickson Park. "Is he okay?" Lilly calls out to the men, breaking the silence. "What are you going to do with him?" she hollers down the hill.

"Yes," zoo man calls back across the steep expanse of the grassy hill. "He's okay. He's going back to the woods."

All three women sigh in unison and watch the truck with the bear drive away and out of sight. They gather up their bags and purses and start down the hill toward the lake just as a two-person camera crew appears from the local TV station. Intentionally, they slow down in order to pass behind the TV camera to listen to the woman talking into the microphone.

"And moments ago, in this very tree…"

"We can watch it on the news," Lulu whispers. "Oh, I'm sorry, you don't have a TV, Lilly."

"Don't be sorry. And Lulu, we saw it live."

"Well, I know, but somehow it seems more real on TV."

Sarah laughs and feels her shoulders loosen and relax. Lilly and Lulu climb down the bank to the lake in an almost reckless manner and both seem almost rowdy, as they maneuver over an old driftwood tree stump. They both want to skip stones and start hunting for good flat skipping stones as soon as they reach the beach. Lilly skips her stones five and six times over the surface of the water, a real pro. Lulu's rocks plunk hard and sink. She doesn't seem to mind. Sarah skips a perfect flat oval stone three times, her best attempt.

"You've got to get down low. Use your wrist," Lilly explains as she flings another stone out over the lake with one hand while holding her sari out of the way with the other. Both Lulu and Sarah try again, but both attempts are sinkers.

"We try too had," Sarah says, but now she's enjoying her sinkers too. She feels like she's throwing away her troubles.

"Oh let's eat, Lulu says, heading for her large basket-like purse. She sits on a big flat rock and takes out a thermos of coffee and a Tupperware container. They find more or less comfortable seats on the large flat granite rocks and Lulu passes out plastic cups of coffee and big wedges of banana bread.

"This is the life," Lulu says, taking a large bite of her bread.

The sky is robin's egg blue and the water a multitude of blues, splashing and hissing against the shore, washing over the sand and small bright stones of the beach. Sarah slips off her shoes and socks and steps into the shallow sandy section of beach. As usual, the lake is freezing cold, but she doesn't mind and finds it refreshing to stand in the cold water as she sips warm coffee. Sarah is not entirely surprised to see both Lilly and Lulu removing their shoes and socks. She steps up to lend a hand to Lulu, who takes tiny steps down from the rock and into the water. Lilly wades right in. The women stand in a row looking out across the water of the lake so wide it seems to have no other side, to have no end. Sarah looks down at their bare feet in the clear icy water and sees six feet, pearly white as fish.

"Sharks!" Lulu yells, and turns toward shore. "Ouch, ouch, ouch! Brrr." She tiptoes out of the water and plunks down beside her purse. Dabbing at her feet with an embroidered white handkerchief, she wiggles her pudgy toes.

"Oh, I just love today," she says.

Lilly and Sarah walk slowly out of the water, fascinated by their now red feet. From the ankles up their legs are white, a distinct contrast to the rosy red of their feet, as though they had been sunburned.

---

BACK IN THE CAR, Sarah holds the sweet pilfered coral and pink roses in her lap. She had been uneasy in the rose garden while Lilly calmly snipped roses and Lulu wandered about humming and poking her nose into the blossoms like a hummingbird. Sarah felt like the lookout at a bank robbery, while Lilly and Lulu were perfectly at ease with their rose rustling. As usual, life with Lilly is a challenge to Sarah. Or maybe it's just plain Duluth.

The women are quiet on the ride up the hill. When they drop Lulu off she smiles after them from her porch and waves with a rose. Lilly drives slowly up the steep hill, and as she turns into her narrow driveway, Rhapsody in Blue comes on the radio. They sit and listen to the Gershwin.

The music washes over them. They haven't sat like this since listening to the monologue on *Prairie Home Companion*, a few weeks ago, just after Sarah moved in with Lilly. Morgan had left for Brazil and their Park Point house was in a state of serious renovation. Then Stephen called out of the blue.

"Well, tell me about Stephen," Lilly says during a quiet section. "Will you see him tomorrow?"

"I think so. At least I told him I would. Just a walk at Chester Park while the leaves are still colorful. " How unfair it seems to her that Stephen's wife is dead. That she died so young. Sarah tenses up, afraid. Lilly is critical of her seeing Stephen, or maybe she's just being critical of herself. Anyway, it's just a walk. She's glad Lilly is quiet, just sitting with her hands on the steering wheel listening to the music. Sarah needs to think things through. Stephen was on her mind when they were standing in the lake. How odd that he would just call like that, out of the blue. He was going on about a book he's working on, something about religious statuary. He's still teaching art history in Minneapolis and said it was the perfect job for him. It was good to hear his enthusiasm, after his loss, though he did not sound quite natural. Maybe he was nervous, calling her.

"Well, let's go in," Lilly says. Her aunt steps inside with the stolen roses and Sarah lingers in the backyard and watches Lilly bustling around in the kitchen. The backyard needs raking; a job for another day. And then there's India. Maybe she should go to India with Lilly like she's been pushing for. And why not now while Morgan is working on his research projects in Brazil and their Park Point house is being restructured. Just the idea of India is enticing. She has always wanted to go to the land of tea and spice, spirituality, monkeys, tigers, the Taj Mahal, crowds and cows and colorful saris and exotic festivals and music. Sometimes when she takes a bath in the evening she pours aromatic oils into the bath water and lights little candles so that when she turns out the light and steps into the dark oily water, she imagines herself stepping into the mysterious waters of the Ganges.

---

THE NEXT MORNING, LILLY FINDS herself in need of a good potato curry salad, her recent invention. She stands at the kitchen sink holding a potato up toward the light, looking it over as she might a piece of sculpture. It's a Yukon gold, and smooth. She holds it delicately, as if it might come to life if she were to be too rough. Lilly's dark hair is streaked with white and held back with a headband that sparkles above the porcelain sink. The deep creases of her dimples make her seem friendly even when deep in thought. Although no longer a young woman, Lilly is attractive. Wearing an apron over her sari and grey wool socks she half skates and half sashays across the floor and hangs her apron beside the beaded curtain of the pantry.

She likes living in her younger sister's house, which is now officially her house, and from the outside a typical Duluth hillside house. But the inside is a bit of India, the country she had written about as a student back in high school that inspired a visit to India where she met her now-dead husband. They had worked on a Peace Corp project together, fallen in love and produced a musician son, Devi, acclaimed sitarist of Bollywood movies who has yet to visit Duluth. *From Duluth to Delhi* was Lilly's first published travel article and now she is as much at home in Duluth as she had been in Delhi.

After her sister died, now some five years past, Lilly moved to Duluth. It seemed the logical solution at the time, coinciding as it did with the accidental death of her husband in India. Her eyelids flutter ever so slightly as she recalls the afternoon of his death by a runaway bus with faulty brakes. So senseless. So sudden. And here too in Duluth, this city built on a steep hill, brakes are a serious matter.

Sarah saunters into the kitchen, accepting the potato her aunt hands her to peel. Lilly smiles and continues to gaze out the window at Lake Superior. Since she's been staying with her aunt she often finds Lilly in a pensive mood in the mornings. Sarah examines the potato, looking for the Buddha her aunt says you can find in every potato. This one has mismatched eyes, a bulgy nose, and a sprout just beginning to grow out of what might resemble an ear. She prefers a potato to be a potato and peels several, dropping them into the cold water of the pot. Lilly has started to hum. She adds a sprig of rosemary and several garlic cloves and talks about suffering; the suffering of mankind, the suffering of the Buddha, the suffering of Jesus, the suffering of potatoes, and the varied forms potatoes are capable of assuming. Sarah brushes a peel from her wrist. She feels like a potato today, lumpy and grey in her old sweat suit and bare feet. She would just as soon have rice. Nothing to peel there.

The kitchen smells of rosemary. Lilly fusses with her spice jars, aligning her favorites: cumin, cardamom, paprika, turmeric and rosemary. She's concerned about Sarah seeing Stephen today, though she is sorry his wife died. And now Stephen is staying with his cousin in Duluth while he works on a book on religious icons. She doesn't see why he can't do that in Minneapolis, or does he just come to Duluth on weekends? So much death these past years. Too much loss. Lilly knows it's not her place to tell Sarah what to do, even if Sarah's brilliant husband, Morgan, spends most of his time in South America living in trees. She likes Sarah's husband, but he is rarely around; usually he is off somewhere doing research. She admires his scientific work for the good of the planet, though she can't see what good he does for his wife. At least Morgan is rich and Sarah has no money worries, even though that luxury has kept her somewhat childish, somewhat immature.

"Where do you get your saris, Lilly?" Sarah asks, touching a pale orange silk shoulder.

"On line. SarisRyou. I'll show you tonight." She recalls the day she bought her laptop from a young man who worked in the produce department at the Kenwood SuperOne. She had reached for some parsley and he almost misted her arm and they had started talking. He brought it up out of the blue, how he had this laptop for sale and he'd give her a good deal. He wanted the money so he could go to Mexico. Said he couldn't face another winter in Duluth. She bought it the next day and never saw the young man again. Lilly pictures him in sunny Mexico, strolling a sandy beach and thawing away his too many winters in Duluth. The computer worked fine, and she found it easy to use and taught herself to send e-mail to Devi in India and how to shop. She's even started writing again.

"Didn't Morgan buy you a new computer?" she asks Sarah, as she turns the heat down under the potatoes.

"It's still in the box. I'll wait until the house is done. I'm on vacation from computers. At least for a while," Sarah says.

# *two*

---

AT CHESTER PARK, SARAH CHOOSES the path that follows the old bobsled trail through the woods to the ski scaffold. It's warm for a northern Minnesota October day. She's wearing a baggy black sweater and Stephen has on a pale fisherman's sweater that would make him invisible in a field of wheat. They walk briskly into the world of trees, far from the cares and duties of their daily lives, and as they walk they slow to a leisurely pace, until they are walking as drifters, seemingly without a care in the world. A confetti of bright leaves fall as they walk: red maple, honey birch, and tiny yellow leaves land in their hair and on their shoulders like miniature goldfish. Sunlight flickers over the forest floor of freshly fallen leaves, gray-green thimbleberry thickets, red-leafed raspberry bushes and hazelnut shrubs.

The only sound is the wind high in the treetops, plus their own voices as they climb the meandering hills through the forest toward the base of the ski scaffolding. The ski jump is visible from many locations in Duluth, but here in the woods they are so close that the trees block their view. As they reach the clearing the ski jump's sudden looming presence gives it a monumental appearance, more like a giant outdoor sculpture, and here in the fall, with no snow, no skiers, and no other people it seems a strangely large item to be in such a private location. Stephen points out two crows squawking at the top of a tall pine at the edge of the clearing. Now that they've stopped walking they are self-conscious in this beautiful and private place. Their silence is almost embarrassing below the raucous cocky crows. They stand awkwardly apart beside the ski jump's high curved slide.

"My father jumped from here," Stephen says. "He jumped on a dare. "He'd never jumped before but once he said he'd do it, well, he was committed, and he did it. Jumped. Right here." Stephen's smile turns to a grimace as they look up the steep slope of the ski jump above them. Looking up at the slide, it doesn't seem like something anyone would actually do. How could a person intentionally push oneself down a dangerously steep slide covered with snow while standing on skis – sticks really, just a couple of well-fashioned boards, at least back then when his father jumped. At this close range ski jumping seems like a bit of fiction for the insane.

Sarah climbed the ski scaffold as a child. She and her friends had summer picnics on the landing on top of the ski jump where they sat cross-legged and munched graham crackers and sipped Coke. She had loved sitting on the wooden ski platform on a warm summer day looking out over the wide blue expanse of Lake Superior, and onto all the little rooftops scattered over the green hills of Duluth. She had thought you could see the whole world from the top of the ski scaffolding.

She and Stephen walk to the edge of the hill from where the skiers soar out into the sky in winter, their arms aerodynamically straight against their sides. She remembered that Stephen's father died when he was young and that his father made cigars in their basement. Maybe he made some of the cigars her father smoked. Funny, she hadn't thought of that before. She imagines his dad looked just like Stephen, a picture of confidence, with curly blond hair, flying out over the hill on skis, a lit cigar in his mouth. How great it must feel, flying through the air on skis, jumping out into the unknown. Into the air like a bird. Like a crazy bird.

They both sigh.

"Landing was the hard part. They had so little room. Just that small space on the other side of the lake," Stephen says.

They look down over the steep grassy slope to the small blue lake below, formed by a dam on Chester Creek. Red maples and yellow birch on the hills opposite the ski jump mirror themselves in the lake, inviting the eye deep into where the trees appear to grow downward, while glistening hypnotically on the water's surface.

"You'd have to be crazy," Sarah says, curious, yet shuddering at the thought of actually ski jumping down there. Stephen raises his eyebrows and looks as if he's about to speak, but then says nothing. "I meant I would have to be crazy," she laughs, becoming more aware of her old friend of long ago, remembering, fascinated once again by Stephen's subtle charms – his smile. She always thought of his lips as a trumpeter's lips because of their sculptural qualities and the thought lingers, making her grope for another thought, a safer thought. After all, here she is, a married woman, out in the woods with an old flame from her college days. But they were adults, reasonable people who shared a reasonable friendship, retained over the past ten years through Christmas cards, and once she even had lunch with Stephen and his wife. She liked her. Shifting her weight toward the balls of her feet, so near the ledge which is pure straight down, a jello-y feeling in her stomach makes her wobble forward for an instant before regaining her balance and stepping back. Disoriented, she is surprised at Stephen's firm hand on her arm.

"You okay?" Stephen asks, releasing his grip on her arm.

"Sure. It's just the height. I stepped too near the edge. I was blurry." She doesn't know what she means by that and he doesn't ask. But what was he thinking. Was he thinking about those long ago days with her? Or about his father? Does he picture his father here? His father's jump was successful, but perhaps Stephen saw that jump as a take off point from which his father flew out into the air, departing from this world on skis, jumping straight out of his life into the other world from this very hillside.

She always saw her own father's departure as from a boat. They were both in Oslo, and she saw her father off at the dock. She was staying on in Oslo, and he gave her a handful of paper Kroner, boarded the Bergensfjord and sailed home to America and back to Duluth, Minnesota. The scene of her father sailing away on the ship is how she pictures his departure from this earth. He looked so dapper in his trench coat, so happy and confident as he boarded the boat. They had waved to each other for a long time as the boat moved away from shore, and she watched the ship until it became small and left the Oslofjord. For Sarah, that was her final image of him, even though she saw him many times again back in Minnesota before his death. How beautiful, this final exit she had chosen for him. For her, he is always a happy sailor at sea. It was on her own return to Duluth that she met Morgan, who had been backpacking in Norway after completing a fellowship year in Geneva.

"Well," she says, and starts walking toward the base of the big ski jump. Stephen follows and they talk about skiing and skating as kids, remembering the horror of frozen feet. The agony after skating or skiing in subzero cold when they would sit with their feet beside a heat register, waiting and dreading the awful pain that would come as their toes thawed out.

"Horrible pain. We probably really were close to frost bite," Sarah says.

"I can't think of anything worse. Well, that's not quite true. I can deal with physical pain," Stephen says.

"It's been two years now, since your wife died?" Sarah asks.

"Two years and two months," Stephen says quietly.

She doesn't know what to say. If he wants to talk about it, she'll listen. They walk closer to the ski jump and Sarah spots an old wooden ladder at the base of the scaffolding. They look at each other. "Want to climb?" she asks.

"Sure," he says stepping forward. A bit surprised at how eager he is, Sarah starts up the old wooden rungs, though the steps look like they belong on the wall of an antique store. Stephen follows once she is high enough to make room. They climb until the ladder is blocked by a wire gate. Backing down, they are both exhilarated by the climb and at the possibilities of life, if they can climb an old wreck of a ladder like that. They walk to the high end of the ski jump and examine the newer stairs to the top and conclude the old ladder was indeed a relic from the past. The skiers used to climb stairs while toting their skis from the landing area by the lake up to the slide, where the ladder led to stairs that followed the edge of the slide straight to the top. The new stairs are out of reach above a metal gate.

They leave the ski jump and cross the clearing toward the path through the woods, now walking a little closer to one another. Stephen talks about his life in Minneapolis and the book he's writing on religious symbols and how he's been visiting churches, looking at stained glass windows and statuary. He says he's been coming to Duluth on weekends for several weeks now. He likes to write on his cousin's balcony overlooking the lake. Sarah listens with surprise. When she was in college he never expressed an interest in religion. Rather the opposite, she had thought, though she did recall that he had been an altar boy as a child. Somehow she connected his being an altar boy with the other experience she knew of his youth, how he had helped his father make cigars in their basement. Cigars seemed religious to Sarah. As a child she watched with intense interest when her father lit a cigar. First the wooden match, then the inhale, and finally the exhale of blue smoke swirling up into the air. Even today she loves the aroma of cigars. Had Stephen now turned religious after the death of his wife?

"Jeannie and I always talked," Stephen said suddenly. "I miss that. She was religious. Quite spiritual, but in her own way."

Sarah pictures a sort of smoking and no smoking area in Heaven, wondering how it would work if you had once smoked but then you quit. Which section would you be in? Would she want to smoke again? Now she can't abide the smell of cigarette smoke, but still finds cigar smoke enticing.

"When someone dies. It changes you," Stephen says. "I mean that's obvious, I know, but you become an entirely different person. Like you've fallen into a mirror and come out the other side and suddenly you're an alien." Mainly it's being alone, he knows, but keeps the thought to himself. He does find the actual church buildings helpful, comforting. When he is listening to the pipe organ on a Sunday morning, he likes the way the sun shines through a stained-glass window. It helps. Sometimes.

"Well, it's beautiful here on a day like this, with all the bright leaves on the trees," Sarah says, thinking of how their fathers could be smoking cigars somewhere in the land of the dead. Wishing you could still burn leaves in the fall, like when she was a kid. That good smell of burning leaves. She feels sorry for Stephen but not too much so. His shoulders seem to sag and shrink in his big sweater as he walks along thinking of death. She's feeling jaunty. She can't help it. It's such a blue-sky day. Perhaps she has a faulty soul. Still, she feels guilty. Jeannie died of lung cancer and had smoked since she was eleven or some crazy really young age.

They stop at the top of the old bobsled run. The wooden runway is long gone, but its pathway is still clearly in use. They walk down the old trail until they come to the bridge over Chester Creek, which is running fast and clear, splashing and bubbling below, past boulders and under a large fallen birch. The wood of the bridge is dark and wet, saturated from last night's rain. Sarah feels the bridge bounce beneath her feet as they walk across. She stops in the center and bounces the bridge intentionally, at first startling herself at what she's doing, and then frightened by how her slight weight makes the bridge bounce considerably, perhaps dangerously. Stephen's quick laughter is the laughter of his devilish past and Sarah glances down at the fast moving water of the river, rather than at Stephen, as they cross to the other side of the bridge.

*His laughter, like water.*

Leaving the bridge, they pass the soccer field that borders the clay tennis courts where they once played together that summer when Sarah was a sophomore in college and Stephen was working on his master's in history. The high fence surrounding the courts is covered with a scarlet curtain of ivy.

As they near the gate, Stephen's off-hand comment about what dreadful courts they were, shocks Sarah. To her, the clay courts were sacred grounds, beautiful and idyllic, surrounded as they were by the hilly northern forest, and with a view of the blue lake below the ski jump. She had loved the clay courts then and she did so now, even though they were no longer maintained and had in fact gone to seed. She had loved running across the soft red clay, so smooth and earthy against the tread of her tennis shoes. The red clay of the court connected her to the earth, and gave her an energy to leap through the air after a tennis ball. She knew tennis players criticized clay as being slow, but it was the extra second, that feeling of time happening that she loved; watching the ball cross the court, the sensation of slow motion and an awareness of space, of depth, as the ball moved through the air. She stood still, remembering how it was, how the ball seemed to float through the air toward her racket, floating through the summer air.

Now here she is, standing in the middle of the old clay court of weeds, chamomile and quack grass poking up through little bumps of soil, and Stephen is standing there waiting for her. Morgan rarely waited for her. If she stopped to adjust her shoe he wouldn't notice she had stopped until he got to the car and even then might not notice until he started the engine. He expected the world to follow him, to keep up. Usually she did.

Stephen was left-handed and a good player. Still, she won plenty of games, though rarely a match. She should have taken lessons, should have developed her serve. Realizing those games, those hours on the courts she had loved were perhaps a trial for Stephen and not a counterpart to her own pleasure at all, she feels the skin on her neck hot with embarrassment. She hadn't been good enough. Yet at the same time, she wanted to leap into the air and shout out loud: The clay courts are still here. Yes!

They walk through the gate from the higher court to the lower court.

"I thought you liked the courts, Stephen," she said, still struggling to comprehend his flippant criticism of the courts where they played every day that summer. "I loved these courts," she says quietly, shuffling her feet down to dig her shoes into the clay, to savor the clay, to reconnect with the past. When they reach the lower gate, Stephen steps through and locks the gate with a click of metal on metal. Sarah is locked in.

"Gotcha," he says through the gate.

She laughs and rattles the gate, playing along, but thinking maybe she liked playing tennis better than she liked Stephen. He opens the gate, says it wasn't really locked anyway, which of course she knew. Walking away from the courts toward the lake, they stop at the sound of a loud rhythmic tapping in the vicinity of the caretaker's house, the old warming house where skiers and skaters warm themselves by the wood-burning stove each winter.

Stephen spots it first. A rare pileated woodpecker, tall with a high red-tufted crest. They watch as it hammers away on the wood of a shed behind the warming house.

Gun shots. Two repeats.

Startled, they whirl toward the explosive bang of the shots, followed by the crackly laugh of an old man standing by the side door of the caretaker's lodge.

"Just scared 'em. Damn crazy birds make holes in my shed."

The old guy walks toward Sarah and Stephen with a rifle slung over his shoulder, humming softly to himself. A thin man, he puts considerable energy and motion into each step, yet his progress is so slow they quickly meet him halfway down the drive.

He squints at Stephen and Sarah. "Birds, spiders, snakes. They all try to get inside. Sign a winter." He takes a crumpled red handkerchief from his pocket and blows his nose. "Leif Larson, pleased to meet you," he says, extending a gnarled hand. They introduce themselves.

Sarah asks about the courts as they walk toward the warming house. Leif tells how his brother-in-law used to take care of the courts and rolled them smooth after a rain with a heavy, barrel-sized metal roller. "It's over there now, that roller is, by the wood pile. Keeps the snow from drifting over the wood. See that stack of birch there?"

"Nice. Fine birch logs," Sarah notes.

"Well, Jake moved to the cities. Got a job making ice. Some kind of truck he drove back and forth over the ice, making new ice. For the rinks. He liked smoothing things out. My sister said he hated even a little wrinkle in his sheets; he'd get up and tighten the sheets, stretch em real tight, military-like. A bit off, if you ask me. Always was. He could whistle good though. Whew, he was always wanting to get on *A Prairie Home Companion* and do his whistling, but then he died. Just up and died."

Leif grabbed his gun and aimed back at the shed, but this time he didn't shoot, just said the word "Bang" and cackled again.

"So, it was nice meeting you Leif," Stephen nods his head, as Leif's hands are occupied with the gun.

"Yes, goodbye Leif," Sarah adds, backing away.

"Right over there, the road by the lake, right where you're headed. Three nuns. I shot straight over their heads. They come down from St. Scholastica sometimes. Couple summers ago. I don't do that anymore. Well, well. Pleased to meet you both. Have a nice day. Real nice day," Leif stands with the rifle on his shoulder and watches as Sarah and Stephen walk down the dirt road toward Stephen's car.

# three

STEPHEN PULLS INTO THE SMOKY TROUT parking lot an hour before dark, as planned. Still, he is ten minutes early, time enough to buy a few smoked fish and get down to the shore on schedule.

The tiny shop looks the same as last time, and it smells the same. The muggy air of the shop is so fishy that as soon as he steps inside he tastes smoked fish at the back of his throat and in his nostrils. Freshly smoked ciscoes, white fish, and lake trout and fresh water salmon lie in cardboard boxes inside the display case. Stephen orders three ciscoes and watches the young woman wrap the fish in newspaper. He finds a curious satisfaction watching this simple folding of newspaper around the fish, a wrapping material and procedure of choice, apparently, for over 90 years. According to the sign by the clock, The Smoky Trout has been in business since 1922. Stephen remembers his father unwrapping smoked fish from newspaper in the kitchen when he was a child. Back then fish parcels were tied in grocery string; now they use a piece of tape. He can see his dad cutting through the delicate bronze skin of the smoked fish. How delicious the pinkish flesh was on crackers. But you had to watch out for bones.

"Is that all, then?" the clerk asks, startling Stephen.

"Oh yes. That's all. No. I'll have some cheese." Stephen adds a hefty chunk of Jarlsberg. "And this too," he says, setting a pound of wild rice beside his package of smoked fish.

"No cheese curds?" she asks.

"No, this is fine," he realizes he needs to get going.

"Okay then, thanks for coming in," she says with a friendly smile. He sees little scratches on her hand and wonders if she ever gets rid of the smell of fish.

Outside, the lake air is breezy and the gulls are squawking. He sets the package of fish beside a can of motor oil in the trunk and drops the bag of rice and cheese into the box his cousin uses for groceries, then walks quickly across the road and makes his way down the bank to the rocky shore of Lake Superior. No one is visible in either direction. He sits down on a rock, but is too restless and decides to walk the beach. A late afternoon sun casts an orangey glow over the beach and across the sky. Stephen laughs, all alone on the beach, noting how the lake looks like a giant smoked fish, with crinkly golden waves, and perfect opal bubbles washing onto the shore. He stands still, admiring the lake, aware that this is the first time he's laughed spontaneously for a long time, though this morning he was quite happy, walking with Sarah, especially when she stomped on the bridge and made it bounce. He doesn't remember her ever doing things like that, anything dangerous or unpredictable.

The sky is red by the time Hawk shows up, surprising Stephen by arriving by boat. Last time they met in the parking lot and made plans to meet at the shore today, but there was nothing said about a boat. He pulls in by a rocky ledge at the edge of the beach. In the shadow of the rock, the silhouette of Hawk and the boat look like a backlit Goya painting. Stephen knows he needs to get over there but his legs feel unmovable and leaden. He is both frozen in place and elated.

He had met Hawk a year ago outside a gas station where he was selling bears carved from logs. They were exquisitely carved and Stephen had thought them nearly museum quality. He bought a small bear for thirty dollars. They guy was talented. It must have been how he hesitated that day, astonished at the quality of the bears made by this seedy looking man. He hadn't known what to say when Hawk asked if there was something else he could do for him. Well, what else do you carve, he'd asked. "Depends," Hawk had said. That's when he got the small St. Francis statue out of his truck and showed Stephen. It looked like a Russian icon, painted in the rich colors of the past. He had especially noted the deep tones with gold edging, and the face. Maybe he carved it himself; maybe it was a real antique. Whatever it was, Stephen wanted it. Hawk said he would sell it to him if he brought a small package to his brother in West Duluth. That's when Stephen's foolishness began. He said yes. Bought the St. Francis and delivered the package to the "brother" who lived above a bar in West Duluth.

Now here he was again, fool that he's become. He feels an adrenalin flush of blood in his face. "Well, here goes." He climbs over the rocks and steps into the boat. When he leaves, he has the sculpture, and the small package for West Duluth, which he tucks into a compartment of mindlessness, which is all he can manage. Hawk, the man of few words who seems to be his new best friend, takes off as soon as Stephen steps ashore.

Stephen feels his heart race as he pulls out of The Smoky Trout parking lot. Once he gets going he knows he'll be okay, with both packages safely in the trunk. There was no one in the parking lot when he came up from the lake. If that girl in the store saw him at all, she only saw someone carrying yet another newspaper-wrapped package. Probably thought he ate his fish down by the shore and had the rest in the newspaper. Didn't look much larger than the ciscoes, not much. Probably she wouldn't think anything. Probably she didn't even see him.

Concentrate on the road and watch for deer. It's dark, yet the moonlight reflected from the lake lights the road as it follows the curves of Lake Superior. Don't even think, just drive. Gigi will be late. She's always late. He'll have a beer, unwind before she arrives. Just a few more miles, forget Hawk, forget the boat, the package. It's getting dark fast, even with the moon rising and clouds drifting in. As he nears the North Shoreline Café, Stephen cringes at the sight of all the cars in the parking lot. At this hour? But of course, it's still dinner time. It doesn't matter, everything looks normal, he's almost sure. It's just nerves.

Gigi waves to Stephen as soon as he steps inside the café. She's with Jeep, the lawyer creep, just what he needs. She rushes over to greet him. No time to unwind and freshen up. There's oil on his boots, and he smells of smoked fish.

"Hey Gigi, how are you?" Stephen says, giving her a cautious hug. Gigi, his beautiful Gigi, though of course she's not his Gigi, not now, never was. Not anyone's Gigi, not even Jeep the Creep's. And here she is, so happy to see him, larger than life, so big and rosy and loud and crazy.

"Oh Stephen, dear Stephen. Stephen Stephen Stephen," she shudders and laughs at the same time in delight.

*Her laughter, like cheap champagne.*

Outrageous, classy Gigi. She kisses his cheek and turns away, allowing her hair to brush across his ear. He wishes he didn't smell like fish, he wishes, wishes. He follows her silk velvet shoulders to their table, where Jeep is talking on his cell phone and scowling at the ceiling.

"Call me when it's ready to go," Jeep says, and drops the phone into his pocket. "So, Richard. How's it going? Been fishing?"

"Stephen. It's Stephen, dear," Gigi corrects him.

Over dinner he studies Jeep. He knows exactly what she sees in Jeep. Money. Or does he know. It's so easy to make quick judgments; he hopes he's wrong and there's a hidden Jeep, a kinder Jeep. The bastard, bringing up the fish smell. Picking at his goat cheese like that, then gobbling his burger like a cannibal. Bet he's like that in court. Stephen is starting to relax, despite the creep. "Stephen, you look at Jeep like he's a leper. Really," Gigi tells him when Jeep leaves for the restroom.

He had thought it was the other way around, but says he has nothing against him, against lawyers. Most lawyers are fine people. Gandhi was a lawyer, J.F.K. "I'm not myself today," he says, dropping a sprig of parsley into Jeep's water glass, which strikes them both as extraordinarily funny, and leads to their inconsolable laughter by the time Jeep returns. He pays no attention to their hysterics.

"I have an extra ticket to *Ski Jump Jubilee* for tomorrow night," Jeep says. "It's yours if you want it. Won't you join me and Gigi? It's completely sold out, has been for a week."

"The Opera. Well, thank you, Jeep," Stephen says, genuinely surprised. "I leave in the morning for Minneapolis, but thanks anyway. I've heard it's terrific. A smash hit original musical comedy opera sort of thing. About skiing, of course, and the history of Duluth, isn't it?"

"Right. It's an operella," Gigi says. "It's wonderful! I saw the first run last spring. Honestly, my stomach and my jaw hurt so bad from laughing I felt like I'd been mugged by a giant talking parrot. Stephen you must see it. A toast to Duluth," she proposes, and they clink glasses and finish off a very nice Merlot.

"Oh no," Gigi says, a look of horror in her wide brown eyes. "The priest's ski robe. It's in the trunk. I promised Anna I'd drop it off. The seam's ripped. I was supposed to sew it up, for the skiing priest. I don't know why I ever joined that costume committee. I don't even know how to sew. Oh God."

"Relax. How long it's gonna take to sew up a seam?" Jeep says, grabbing her hand and running his fingers up and down her arm.

"They need it for tomorrow night. Good Lord, what if I hadn't remembered. It's a priest's long brown robe, but short enough for skiing or skating" she explains. "Stephen, do you think you could take the priest's robe, whatever they call it –

frock? No, that doesn't sound right, does it?" She laughs a hiccupy sort of laugh. "We're going to Thunder Bay tonight and we'd have to drive all the way back to Duluth, and then back north again. And with the deer at night jumping out of the woods . . . ."

"Sure, I'll take it. You know, I think I know someone who could use that ticket. I think you know her. Sarah Salveson – now Sarah Morgan?"

"What?" Gigi asks, setting her wine glass down so hard people from other tables turn to look. "Sarah's still in Duluth? I guess we lost track of each other when I got married and left Duluth. Well, before I got back. Two Ex's ago. Something like that. Sarah is absolutely wild, but you'd never know it. She's my exact opposite. She's as quiet as I am loud. This is great! We used to go to little cafes and read poetry. She'd tell these amazing stories she'd just make up on the spot. I'd smoke cigars. Tiparillos."

Gigi tells how she and Sarah wore black and looked cool and read avant-garde poetry: Howl, French poetry, in French, of course, and sometimes they read their own poetry. "We were outrageous. Or thought we were. Then she married a banker. I met him once. He was kind of stiff, not what I expected for Sarah at all," Gigi shakes her head, remembering how good looking he was. "Very smart though. He's something else too. Maybe a scientist. Or an explorer. Do we still have explorers? Maybe he's not a banker. It must have been the family was in banking. Yes, that's it."

"Morgan. I think I know the guy. Maynard Morgan, isn't it? From the Morgan family. Railroads. And mining," Jeep says. "Some connection with horses too, I seem to recall."

"No, Jeep. That's Morgan horses," Gigi says, and Stephen can't tell if she's being factual or rude to Jeep.

Stephen is somewhat embarrassed that he doesn't know any more about Morgan than they do, except now he knows that he goes by his last name. He's restless, and suggests they give him the priest's robe and information he needs to deliver it to the costume designer. Jeep insists on paying the bill. There's no arguing with a lawyer.

Outside, looking into the trunk of Jeep's car, Stephen finds himself stuttering as he replies to Gigi's questions about the address in Duluth. He's never known himself to stutter. Never. It's the priest's robe, lying there crumpled up in the dark trunk next to their luggage and a large antique-looking ice fishing spear. Too weird. All he can think is that it looks like murder. Like a priest has been murdered and this is all that's left of him. Are they putting him on, about the opera, the costume? And how does one get mugged by a large talking parrot? He knows he is sometimes gullible. But of course he has the ticket. Crazy. Crazy thinking.

Stephen dutifully takes the priest's robe and folds it into a neat square before setting it inside the trunk of his cousin's car. He hears Gigi and Jeep arguing as he drives off toward Duluth. There's no reason for him to be so tired, it's not that late, but he's exhausted. Stephen concentrates on the road, assigning himself the single-minded task of getting to Duluth without hitting a deer.

Just outside the city he stops for gas, checks the address of where he's to drop off the priest's robe, and eats a Reese's peanut butter cup whole while looking up the phone number for Sarah's Aunt. Easy name to remember: Lilly Marlene. Nine, ten, eleven, twelve. He hasn't heard so many rings in years, and he listens in a kind of trance. This Aunt Lilly seems to be the only person he knows without an answering machine, he doesn't actually know her, but he'd like to meet her.

He'll drop off the priest's robe first, then make the West Duluth delivery where normal time doesn't exist. Delivering the priest's robe to Anna, the costume designer, he feels like an actor, and not at all himself. In fact he finds himself speaking with just a touch of an Irish brogue as he explains about the robe. "Glad to be of assistance," he tells her as she takes the robe with an elegant gesture, as if receiving the robe of a king. She doesn't seem surprised that the hem hasn't been sewn up. Behind her are several bolts of material stacked on a piano bench, and three dressmaker's dummies look like aliens in the dim light of the room. He didn't know they still made those things. "Bit of Irish whiskey, that's what I'll be needing," he says to himself, quietly, but distinctly, as he takes the steep steps down to his car. He didn't mind the wide-eyed curious look Anna had given him as he left. One mission completed.

On the way to West Duluth he decides he's in Act Two of a play and he's been assigned the role of a petty criminal, despite his good inner self. However did Hawk take that chance with him that day he bought the bear? He could have gone straight to the police. Stephen knew what he was getting in for, what he was to deliver. When he'd asked Hawk about that early meeting he had just said "I know people. That's my gift. That and art. Making good sculpture."

Climbing the dirty stairwell, his nerves are raw. The guy, he doesn't know his name and doesn't want to, opens the door. The apartment smells sad. They exchange packages, and the door slams with an ugly thud as he starts down the stairs and past a bag of rancid trash at the landing.

His cousin is asleep when he lets himself in and he hears Jim snoring over the sound of the radio on his way to the bathroom. Showering, trying to wash off the fish, the guilty slimy feeling, he scrubs hard, but it's still there, of course, as he towels off, knew it would be, and he dreads the night of dreams ahead. He falls asleep hard.

# *four*

THE ENVELOPE ADDRESSED TO SARAH is sticking out of the mail slot when Lilly steps outside for the morning paper. She props it against the African violet on the kitchen table and heads back to bed with her toast and coffee. The crossword puzzle seems easy this morning and she is particularly pleased at being able to use the word Ganesha, one of her favorite Indian deities. She makes a mental note to look for a small likeness of this elephant-headed deity on her trip – a lucky omen, surely, finding this word in her crossword.

Sarah knocks on Lilly's already-opened bedroom door. "Morning, Aunt Lilly," Sarah says, yawning. "Hmm, the coffee smells good. I had a really weird dream and now I feel – happy, actually."

"Yes?"

"Oh, there's hardly anything left of it, except this sort of euphoria. But I know that I'm going to India someday, but just not this year."

Lilly pats her newspaper like a pet and invites Sarah to sit down. "I'd like to teach yoga while you're in India," she tells Lilly. "A small class, if I could use your meditation room, which would be perfect. I wonder what Morgan is doing this morning," she ponders. "What kind of jelly is that? Chokecherry, I hope,"

"Yes, from those berries by the garage. And of course you can use the big room, provided you teach me too when I get back. The Persian carpet can be rolled up and stored in the back."

Sarah is buttering her toast when the Federal Express man knocks on the door. She tucks the package under her arm and joins Lilly with her breakfast tray. "Lilly, I'm going to have your doorbell fixed while you're in India. More coffee?"

"Yes, please. And one sugar lump. I don't think the doorbell is fixable. It's an antique."

"You need a new one, with a chime. Yum, I love this bread," she says finishing the last bite and opening the package which contains a CD from Morgan. The label reads: Monkeys and Parrots, October 5. Last time it was shorebirds. She reads the letter, what there is of it.

*Dear Sarah. All is going well here. See you soon in a few weeks. Moving to the boat outside Rio in a few days. Will call. Love, Morgan,* she reads. He signs off with a smiley face with a moustache. She hands Lilly the letter.

"So he does have a bit of a creative side, there with the moustache." No personal comments to speak of, she notes. "Suppose it's hard to shave when you're in a tree."

She'll have to buy a CD player to hear the CD. The old one is buried in a box down at the Park Point house, impossible to find now. She can use it in her yoga class too. She likes to use music in her classes. Lilly doesn't like recorded music, at least not in the house. She loves music, as long as it's live. Recorded music or monkeys on a CD, it's all destructive to the soul, according to Lilly. False and unreal. Sarah finds that she sings to herself more here at her aunt's, and hearing Lilly singing or humming as she goes about her day is relaxing. There is something good about her natural ways, but she is not the purist she thinks she is. Buying saris online and watching "Slumdog Millionaire" the other night at Lulu's. And then she listens to the radio in the car.

She liked the CD Morgan sent of ocean sounds and shorebirds. Of course Sarah can hear all the seagulls she wants any old day down by the lake, so she was puzzled by that one.

Maybe he was trying to connect, in his own way. Or she was supposed to notice subtle differences in the gulls of Lake Superior and those from the Brazilian coast. She did try that but had more fun just watching sandpipers run along the lake shore.

Lilly brings up the pheasant, which has been on her living room wall for nearly a year. Sarah bought the stuffed bird at a yard sale just outside of Two Harbors and rode back to Duluth with the pheasant on her lap. It's for her brother in New York, but she can't decide how to get it there. No one drives that far, nor wants a pheasant on their lap on a plane, even if she could get it through security. Last summer when she called Tom Troll, he said birds are the hardest to ship because the heads tend to come off. She didn't want that. But he did say he would pack it for her and wire the head in place.

"I'll take it over to Troll's Taxidermy and have it shipped," she tells her aunt. That place has been on Sixth Avenue since before she was a child. It seems to her like something out of the twilight zone, with its old-fashioned grey-green siding and big sign with Old English lettering. She lifts the pheasant down from the shelf. It's lighter than she remembered.

Lilly is chanting and rinsing out the teacups. Sarah stands and listens at the kitchen door, still holding the pheasant and unconsciously petting its feathers. The bird seems like a bird of India, now with Lilly chanting; with its patterns and swirl of coppery colors it seems like a bird who might sip chai and strut about behind beaded curtains.

She sets the pheasant on a side table and goes out the backdoor. First she needs to rake. In the garage, she spots her dad's old wooden skis up in the rafters. This is one of the things she likes about Duluth, how her own history is everywhere. It's reassuring, seeing the skis up there in the same place they've always been. And the lake is like that too. It's always there, no matter where you go, a constant presence visible from most everywhere in this city on a hill. She sees it framed by the window of the garage like an abstract blue painting, and again in its fullness when she steps out into the yard, rake in hand. Lake Superior, as beautiful and old as the moon, still visible this morning as a pale crescent above the Mountain Ash beside the driveway. Leaning on the rake she watches a crow fly below the moon, a dark accent that flies out of view. How many moons have shone down on the lake over the years? Years and years of moons, thousands of moons. And now these leaves. It's warm again today. Another warm October morning. Time seems to fall away and though unaware of having raked, she finds herself surrounded by several tidy piles of leaves. She fills a large yard basket and hauls it in the wagon to the compost heap at the base of the old birch. Down in the ravine the water of the creek is flowing slowly and she can hear its steady gurgling.

After a quick call to Tom Troll, she is ready for the taxidermist. Standing in front of Lilly's house with the pheasant tucked under her arm, she feels like a Kindergartner on the way to Show and Tell, especially with Aunt Lilly waving at her from the doorway. It's another Indian summer day; no reason to drive such a short distance. Better to take a stroll with the pheasant, take it for a walk, even if it is dead, as it begins its journey to New York. Her brother already has a stuffed duck in his office, and soon this bright plumed bird will hang beside the duck on the wall. Under the sun, the pheasant's feathers are dazzling, and bright as the fall leaves of the maples she walks beneath. She is excited about the start of its journey to New York, assured this morning by her brother that if the head comes off, he'll mend it. After all, he is a doctor.

She has complete faith in him, just as she did when he operated on her dolls long ago when they were children. He told her later that he wanted to practice his stitching, but at the time she believed he was saving their lives. And how fortunate her dolls were, to have a twelve-year old doctor-to-be so readily available to remove an appendix, or perform a bit of brain surgery. She didn't mind the large black stitches, which he never removed; her dolls were serious dolls, brave survivors worth saving and mending and to her it seemed normal to put dolls to bed with the Frankenstein scars of their various surgeries.

Although no one else is out walking, Sarah feels self-conscious with the pheasant under her arm as she nears her old grade school, and the same school her parents attended. She still has the SuperOne grocery store bag in her pocket and slides it over the bird's head and torso but quickly slips it off and stuffs it back in her pocket. The tail is too long. She might as well let the bird have a taste of fresh air, even if it is dead. Maybe it will get something out of it. Who's to say a trace of its spirit doesn't still linger in the feathers. Can you divide a soul into fragments? A bit here, a bit there? Still, it feels good strolling along in the fall with the bird and Sarah starts to sing: "Oh what a beautiful morning, Oh what a beautiful day."

School is in session and she can see kids moving about in the first floor classroom that used to be her Kindergarten. Now the school specializes in foreign languages. She wants to listen in and hear what language the children are speaking in the old classroom. Spanish? French? German? Maybe Italian, or Russian? Wouldn't that be something, in the school where her dad said they practiced air raid drills out in the halls and had to kneel down and tuck their heads until the teacher gave the all clear. "My dear bird," she says patting the bird gently. "How things change." In her own day they had a big wooden slide in the middle of the Kindergarten room, though she missed out on Ms. Ricky's friendly black dog her brother knew. That dog had attended Kindergarten for ten years and retired with Ms. Ricky, a year before Sarah started school.

Grant School is a three-story brick building, a well-built school much the same as it had been with the exception of the extension to the gymnasium. She had been the only girl who could walk the entire circumference of the school along the narrow ledge that circled the school. Regarding physical matters she was a dare devil with a trapeze artist's sense of balance. "Oh well, just as well I didn't join the circus like I wanted to back in fifth grade," Sarah says, and sighs, leaving the school behind. Remembering and walking with the bird as a companion, the day feels friendly. Even the cement sidewalk with its familiar cracks seems sociable and she knows she's smiling to herself like one of those odd balls she sometimes sees talking to themselves downtown.

She passes Johansen's Bakery and soon turns the corner to Sixth Avenue. The old sign for Troll's Taxidermy is immediately visible, its weathered sign much the same as years ago. On the phone, Tom Troll said she should use the side door. She knocks.

"Come in."

Stepping inside is like stepping back in time and Sarah is immediately disoriented. Tom Troll takes the bird with a little ceremonial bow. She answers questions about the bird's history mechanically. No, she doesn't know how old it is, only that it had been in a store in Minneapolis before she bought it at the sale near Two Harbors one summer. Tom's workroom is warm and inviting, with a hint of freshly-brewed coffee, and birch wood crackling in the stove; not anything like the unwholesome place she was expecting.

Birds, deer, and fish all seem to be observing Tom and Sarah, including her pheasant, now already settled on the wall above the work bench. Sarah is aware of many sets of curious glass eyes, yet it is not unpleasant but instead downright friendly in a peculiar sort of way. All of the dead stuffed creatures have a hominess about them, and it is as though she has entered an enchanted cottage in the middle of a northern forest and she realizes how well the name Tom Troll, suits its owner.

Tom explains how he will thread a wire through her pheasant's head and body and fix its wobbly head with a bit of epoxy. Before shipping, he will screw the driftwood stand to the crate. The workshop is distracting her attention from Tom's explanations and she is craving a cup of coffee from the enameled pot sitting on the wood-burning stove. It smells extraordinarily delicious. Her father had one of those blue Lumberjack coffee pots like Tom's – a watery blue with white speckles like a bird's egg. He used it for camp coffee. But what was heating in those tin cans at the back of the stove? Glue? Beans? Some strange stew? Her desire for coffee evaporates. Tom is filling out a form and misses Sarah's momentary shudder.

"Federal Express comes on Friday; she'll be ready to go," Tom tells her, smiling up from the paperwork.

She hasn't been as attentive as she should have been so she hopes she hasn't missed anything important. But this is good. Finally it'll be on its way. She tells Tom she really likes his workroom. Studio? There is so much to look at and wonder about.

Just what is inside that large white freezer across from the stove? Frozen pizza? Dead pizza? Bambi? All of the above probably. And those white plastic deer heads hanging in such a neat row above the freezer. How does he transform them into such life-like creatures? Are they all deer manikins or are some antelope and elk? Are those ghostly shapes just waiting for Tom Troll to bring them to life, to give them eyes, give some meaning to the Styrofoam heads?

On the wooden floor, a hide the size of a coyote is spread over newspapers, fur side down. A few bright red spots indicate how newly dead and separated from its body the animal is. Yet even this seems not totally gruesome, or not too gruesome. Tom is so kind, like the shoemaker in a Hans Christian Anderson story. Sarah looks into the eyes of a black bear at the back of his work bench. Tom is smiling at her like a northern Buddha, and invites her to stop in again. "To see the animals," he says, as he walks her to the door.

"Tom, you're a magician," she tells him as she leaves the shop, thanking him for his help with the pheasant. She tells him, yes, she would like to come back with her camera some time.

---

IT MAY HAVE BEEN she was bewitched by the animals in Tom Troll's taxidermy shop when she crossed Sixth Avenue, or it may have been the driver was simply blinded by the light as he turned onto the avenue. Later, in the hospital, Sarah remembered leaping away toward the curb and the dark red metal front of the car that tossed her though the air. She remembered part of the license plate: 420. She told Tom to write it down. It was the first thing she said. She could only get the first three numbers but she didn't want to forget them. When she rose to her feet the pain had been such a shock. Tom helped her cross the street to his shop where she slid awkwardly into a big easy chair while he called 911. "Yes, I wrote it down, 420," he told her while he waited for the operator. She could see his hands shaking. She wanted to stay with the birds and the deer. Even the fish. Even the poor dead bodiless coyote on the floor. It was nice and warm and quiet. *No siren, no ambulance, please. Just let me sleep by the wood burning stove. So warm here; so safe.*

Sarah awoke surrounded by white curtains and silence. She was still at the edge of a dream, and a parrot chattered away while she shook her head at the bird until it understood she wanted to hear opera. The parrot was a marvelous tenor, much like Pavarotti. But the aria, was it from *Don Giovanni* or *Tosca*? She must remember.

"Hello. I'm Carol, your night nurse. How are you? On a scale from one to ten, how's your pain?" she asks, smiling kindly.

Sarah tries to move, but stops abruptly, stunned at the pain in her back. "It feels like I was hit by a sledge hammer, a huge sledge hammer, and like someone's put hot coals inside my spine."

"Would that be a ten then?"

"Yes, ten."

The nurse pats the bedding and tells Sarah she'll be back with something to make her more comfortable. Sarah notices a plastic tube taped to her arm. Some of it comes back. Being rolled down the hall and looking up at the ceiling. She told someone they needed pictures on the ceiling. Then sliding into a large machine that looked like a giant sewing machine and a voice from another room telling her to breathe in and hold her breath. Over and over and something about smaller slices. And another room and another metal table and big machines on the ceiling that looked like torture devices. She had laughed though, and told someone she had seen this in a Laurel and Hardy movie. They were stretching Laurel and shrinking Hardy. Or the other way around. Then another room, much like a cave with no light though it seemed this would be the one with the light at the end. She was crying and was not to move; hold her breath, breathe, hold it.

"Have a cracker." The nurse holds out a pill and a glass of water with a bent straw. "Best to eat a little something with the pills." The nurse was kind and said she was lucky, that she would be fine. Two compression fractures in her spine. No paralysis. She would be just fine. Yes, she thought she could sleep now, and yes, she would push the buzzer if she needed anything. Compression fractures. So serious, so painful.

Sarah wanted to talk to someone but knew she couldn't call Aunt Lilly in the middle of the night. No one wants calls in the middle of the night. She must know though; probably Lilly had already been here. That's who she would have told them to call. In the dark it is hard to tell the time; it is either 2:30 or 3:30 a.m.

Morgan is probably unreachable, still somewhere in the jungle sleeping under mosquito netting. Or in a boat. He used to invite her along but she never cared to join him after that one trip to Peru, and then he stopped inviting her. "Sleeping on a boat," she says aloud, and is immediately alarmed at her slurred speech. "Did I injure my brain," she says, testing her voice again, which is still slurred, and almost undecipherable. Brain damage? She reaches toward the night button to call the nurse, to ask about her brain, her speech, when she sees Aunt Lilly's tiny traveling brass Buddha on her nightstand shining reddish gold from the call button's red glow. Letting her arm fall back to the bed, suddenly drowsy, she closes her eyes and falls asleep.

---

A DROWSINESS HANGS OVER the sleepy patients of the orthopedic ward as morning arrives at the hospital. Nurses walk leisurely down the halls in pastel colors as if in a quiet garden at dawn and the only sounds are their soft voices and the tinkling of breakfast dishes as hospitality carts turn corners delivering cornflakes, bacon and eggs, toast and coffee.

Sarah wakes to the smell of bacon, an aroma that makes her nauseous. She turns to her side, moving inch by inch, until she's sitting on the edge of her bed. She reaches behind her, expecting to feel raw bones poking through her skin but instead feels normal smooth skin. She ties the ends of her pale gray robe, wondering how anyone could choose such a hopeless material for a hospital gown – the gray of dirty walls and embellished with tiny green forks. What could they have been thinking? She shudders at the gown, yet is pleased she is aware enough to note this fashion disaster. She can stand. One step and then the next; she finds the tiny bathroom, equipped with hand rails and an odd tub or shower facility with no shower curtain. Her internal plumbing still seems to be working. When she returns to the bed a nurse scolds her. "You call me next time. Don't go getting up by yourself now. Are you okay?"

"I think so," she says, sitting down slowly. Feet up, then roll slowly into place like a log, the nurse tells her. No bending." Her name is Carrie, and not the nurse she saw in the middle of the night. Carrie tucks her in and shows her how to make the head of the bed go up and down, and she is ready to send it up and down, up and down, like Homer, in the Simpson's cartoon. "Bed goes up, bed goes down. Bed goes up, bed goes down." Alarmed at her craziness, what is she doing saying this aloud? But her speech is clear, not at all slurred like it was in the night.

A small serious group of people moving in unison, a few with notepads, enter her space and the tallest one pulls back the curtain surrounding the bed all the way open. They introduce themselves as doctor this and doctor that, and their names float off like feathers. One doctor asks questions while he looks at the ceiling. She looks up at the ceiling too but sees nothing but a white ceiling. No spiders, no charts, no escaped seagulls from the lake or parrots from last night's dream.

She pushes her foot against the doctor's hand when he tells her to resist. Then the other foot. She can do this and is also able to resist each shin appropriately against the hand on cue. This is good, he tells her. "You have two compression fractures," he says. "Yes?" she asks, seeking a further explanation. A doctor in a gray suit steps close and says it means her back is broken in two places. He gives her a big smile as he delivers this news. Still, she prefers his straight-forward language. This doctor in the gray suit has a big nose which gets bigger as he leans forward and he nods in a kindly way as he rocks back and forth, the nose coming and going, enlarging and receding, as he totters, appearing out of focus to Sarah, like he's doing a toothpaste commercial on TV where the person's face looms large and out of focus, especially the nose – a real Jimmy Durante nose. But she likes his smile. He's nice, even if he has bad news about her broken bones. He seems like an entertainer, someone from vaudeville days. Dr. Nose, she'll call him. The one who looks at the ceiling can be Dr. Ceiling. She's pretty sure the others are students, the younger ones with the notebooks: interns accompanying the masters on rounds. They all leave before Dr. Nose has a chance to tell any jokes or do a magic trick. He winks just as the nurse slides the curtain closed and the funny morning horror comedy show ends.

Sarah experiments with various position for the head of the bed by raising the level a few inches up or down and settles on something between lying down and sitting up as the most comfortable.

The phone rings and she's ready to answer, but a voice from the other half of the room answers from behind the bed curtains.

No, this is Marie," the voice says. "No, I'm not Sarah."

I'm Sarah," Sarah calls out through the curtain. "Maybe they want me." Sarah finds the number for her phone for Marie. "He'll call back," Marie tells her but she doesn't know who it was. Sarah and Marie introduce themselves through their respective curtains. Marie's breakfast arrives.

Sarah raises her bed expecting that her breakfast will follow too. Sarah's phone rings. It's her brother from New York. They can hardly hear each other and she has to shout. She tells him about the compression fractures and he says she'll be shorter now. This makes her laugh. What else can she do? She was already short, only 5'2". He says she needs 1300 grams of calcium a day and she should look at labels. If a container of yogurt contains fifty percent of her daily need for calcium, she should take off the percent and add a zero and she'll have 500 grams of calcium so she would need 700 more for that day. She feels peaceful hanging up the phone. He always makes her feel everything will be okay, even if she is

44

shorter now. She forgot to mention the pheasant but that's all right. He'll be all the more surprised when it arrives, unless Aunt Lilly already told him.

A new face peeks through the curtains. "Hello, I'm Carol. How are you doing?"

"Okay. Sore."

"How's your pain?"

"Seven and a half, when I move," Sarah says, feeling she's catching on to the hospital lingo. This could be applied to anything, happiness for instance. She considers asking the nurse how her day is going, on a level of one to ten. Carol looks so radiant and optimistic. She promises to return with some nice pain pills. Sarah sinks back against her pillow and spots a menu tucked into the side of her swivel tray. Omelet, cereal, toast, juice. Everything sounds good. She wants it all. A young woman comes to wheel out Marie's dishes and Sarah asks when she'll get her breakfast. Someone will call her, the woman tells her; she can't do anything herself. She smiles and pushes the cart out the door, and Sarah covets an uneaten slice of toasted bread left on a plate, considering how delicious it would be with strawberry jam, or Lilly's chokecherry jelly. "Couldn't I just have some toast and coffee?" she calls out to the woman.

"You have to order on the phone. I just deliver," she apologizes.

Forty-five minutes pass and no one calls to take her breakfast order. A call to the nurse doesn't help. She is told someone will call her. Soon the phone rings and she hears Marie answer. "No, I'm fine," Marie says. "I already ate."

"No, that's for me, my breakfast," Sarah calls out, but Marie insists it was for her.

Seems to be a phone mix up, Sarah decides, and wonders if they'll also get one another's medicine. She hopes Marie isn't having her leg amputated. Sarah tries the phone number on the back of the menu. She gets through and is told she is on a liquid diet and cannot have food because she may be scheduled for surgery.

"No, no. They aren't going to operate. Dr. Ceiling said so," she insists. "She's only getting a back brace." The pain pills – Carol gave her two – so strong. She's slurring her speech again. She didn't mean to say Dr. Ceiling. Now they'll think she's out of it and she won't get any toast. "I'm not on liquids. I can eat. I need breakfast. I need toast?" she almost shouts, trying hard to enunciate clearly but it comes out like a big blur, one long nonsensical word.

She is told they will talk to her nurse and call her back. Sarah falls asleep as soon as she hangs up the phone.

---

MORGAN STRIDES ALONG THE CORRIDOR past the hospital's main floor lobby in his fatigues and outback hat. He follows the signs, turning with abrupt right angles at each corner. He steps into the elevator in his knee high boots and with precision, pushes the button to the fifth floor. A nurse gets on at the fourth level. At the ring of the elevator bell on five, Morgan announces "C sharp," more as a general comment than as one to the nurse, though by the time she thinks of a response he is far down the hall. She closes her mouth, wondering who he could be. An actor? Such peculiar clothing, even for Duluth, far more appropriate for a safari.

Sarah is asleep when Morgan is shown to her room. He winces at the sound of a soap opera coming from a TV in the far half of the divided room as he peers in past the curtains of his wife's room. Sarah, his lovely sleeping beauty. He turns abruptly to catch up to the nurse who showed him to the room. First he needs to get Sarah moved to a private room, and she must have a view of Lake Superior. And music. Good music.

"La Belle. I'm here. Here we go."

"Morrie?" Sarah finds her bed being rolled down the hall with her husband leading the way with pomp and haste, directing all traffic to step aside for the procession of his wife on her way to her room with a view. "Where are we going?" she asks, trying to raise her head, wondering if she's having a heart attack or profuse internal bleeding and is being rushed to an operating room.

She hears an unusual chanting type of music as soon as they turn the corner and wheel her into the private room. The room has a sensational view of the lake. Lake Superior looks enormous and the panoramic view of the blue outside world startles Sarah after her closet-like existence of the past twenty-four hours, or however long it's been, she can't tell.

"Much better," Morgan says, looking around the room appreciatively before coming to kiss Sarah's hand. Sarah laughs out loud at this gallant and old-fashioned greeting from her jungle-scientist husband. How weird. How perplexing. Morgan kissing her hand? He's never done that before. Is her hospital bed floating in some topsy-turvy dream land? Morgan looks serious, yet she can't help laughing. Still, she would never laugh if it weren't for the pills, but Morgan acts as if her laughter is normal. Shouldn't Dr. Nose be here too? Her vaudeville doctor with the smiling bad news? She looks around the room.

"Do you like it?" Morgan asks, looking to the lake. She raises her bed and sees an ore boat leaving the harbor. "Oh, an ore boat. Yes. I like seeing the lake. I can breathe better now. What is that music? When did you arrive? Did Lilly call you?" Sarah notes the pleats of his shirt front, and the flap of a large tear in the sleeve of his camouflage jacket which reveals the white of a tuxedo dress shirt. Noting her glance, Morgan smoothes the torn material of his jacket into place. It falls open as soon as he removes his hand. "I was in the tree lab. But I came right down. Yes, it was Lilly who called," he tells her. It tells her about the music. It's indigenous music for fish; a type of chanting to celebrate for all the fish in their nets. Kind of an homage to the fish – a song of thanksgiving, he says. Morgan sits on the edge of Sarah's bed, nodding and drumming on his knees to the beat of the fish chant, recalling the scene where he recorded the native music, the faces lit by fire light, the gourds of white beer and the circle dance going on and on late into the night below a big yellow moon. Just when Sarah is considering how this is life as usual; Morgan being both here and there, he turns to her and strokes her uncombed hair.

"Hello," Aunt Lilly says, smiling at them from the door. "Breakfast."

"Oh, I'm starving. I couldn't get anything to eat. There was some confusion with the phones. Mine wasn't working – I could hardly hear. I think my roommate, Marie, or the one before her, well someone switched the phones – the cords were all tangled up. It's just silly. What did you bring?" she asks, sitting at attention and pulling her tray across the bed, ready to eat and happy with Morgan and Lilly here and her view and glad she didn't end up having an operation Marie was supposed to have.

"Curried lentils and lefse. Here you go. It's still hot. Rhubarb sauce, in this little one." Sarah starts eating and Lilly pours three glasses of chai.

"It's hot," Lilly says, handing Morgan his glass. "Sarah likes sandpipers. Did you know that?"

"Sandpipers. I did not know that. La Belle, this is something new?" Morgan looks mortified.

"Oh, not to eat," she says, somewhat confused. "I mean their song. I like to hear them sing, if I could remember. And how they run along the sand," she says seriously.

A nurse comes with a menu and two pills for Sarah. She tells the nurse she's a seven and Morgan asks about the pills and takes notes in a small leather notebook.

"And I'd like to hear *The Magic Flute,*" Sarah says between bites. "And *Tosca.*"

"Well yes, at the Met, when you're better," Morgan says.

"Yes, that too, but just a CD for now. It'll help me relax. Lilly this is delicious."

"Sandpipers and *Tosca.* All right. And *Die Zauberflote.* Yes," Morgan says.

"Wait! Young lady," he rises to follow the nurse. "When can she go home?"

The nurse doesn't know; he'll have to talk to the doctor.

---

MORGAN AND LILLY are gone and Sarah is barely awake and resting on her back. An attractive young woman in jeans wearing a neon pink T-shirt, her upper arms ringed with bracelets of tattoos, stands at the doorway to her room. Jessie's hair is a striking combination of lavender, violet and mauve.

"Is she dying," Jessie asks the nurse.

"Oh no. She injured her back. Hit and run."

"How terrible. But there's something about her. Very pleasant aura. What's this room? Beaded curtains in a hospital room? Is that a sari she's wearing? It looks like a sari."

"It's the family. They brought all that stuff, and the incense. I rather like it, myself."

"Me too. I could do her hair," Jessie says.

By the time Morgan returns with the *Tosca* CD, Jessie has finished and left for the day and Sarah is twining the cerulean blue streaks in her hair into a braid.

"My new blue hair," she says, and tells him about Jessie and how she's trying to improve her Karma by doing good deeds because she was a mean boss in a car factory in her previous life, a Ford plant in Flint, Michigan. Now she's married to a tattoo artist here in Duluth, and does hair. She has a friend in Minneapolis who went to California to learn how to bond hair," Sarah says, holding out the blue strands of hair. She tells him how Jessie just walked into her room and opened a fishing tackle box full of brightly colored hair, which she knew wasn't for making fishing flies, because Jessie's hair was an explosion of shades of lavender that flowed down her back. She pulled up a chair and asked Sarah to choose a color. It happened so quickly she hardly had a choice, except to pick from purple, lavender, green, or blue. "Jessie bonds it with a special iron so it's part of your hair," she says. "It just took a few minutes to do three sections, and I think it looks natural, don't you? Jessie said it goes with my aura."

"Very blue. It is quite a natural blue, that's true. Much like a Steller's jay, or a western jay, yes. No. It's the blue of the banded cotinga, an amazing bird, nearly hunted to extinction for its feathers. Ah, La Belle." Morgan kisses her, carefully, and asks where the hair comes from. She explains how some women in India cut their hair when they get married and that's what they use, that it's real hair, not her hair dyed blue. She can wash and comb it. It's soft. She wonders whose it is, was.

He takes an envelope from his pocket and hands it to her. She isn't sure about the handwriting on the envelope. It looks vaguely familiar but it's definitely not Morgan's. It's a ticket for the opera, for last night, from Stephen. "A gift from Gigi's boyfriend," she reads, from the yellow sticky note attached to the ticket. "I haven't seen Gigi for years. I wonder if she still smokes cigars." She hands Morgan the ticket.

Shamans sometimes smoke cigars, he tells her, leaning closer to look at the blue streak in her hair, which he examines solemnly. "It is soft," he says in a whisper. "What is Stephen doing these days?"

"Stephen? He's working on another book. Something on Christian symbols and what different cultures do with them. He would be interested in the Shamans who smoke cigars. Smoke is a symbol of the spirit world, don't you think? Why are you wearing a tuxedo shirt?"

He seems embarrassed, and explains that Lilly called the embassy. He had been in the tree with his night camera when Kila climbed up with the news. He was stunned. "I just could not believe it. I didn't want to believe it was true, that you had been hit by a car. Terrible news." Kila stayed in the tree and I took the boat into town, and then I had only the one clean shirt which I was saving for the fundraiser next week at the embassy. But I'm staying here. Right here," he says, patting the bed.

"Are you staying at Lilly's," she asks. But he's staying at the Radisson tonight and then is moving to the Lakefront Inn so he can walk the beach. He says he'll look for sandpipers for her. "Look, there's another boat coming in."

Sarah raises her bed as far as it will go. They watch a wide gray ship near the harbor and listen to the whistle calls of the bridge and the boat. Two longs and a short from the boat, then two longs from the bridge. She studies the lake with the intensity of her pain killing drugs which allow for no distractions, only a single-minded concentration on the many shades of blue. At the horizon the lake is a dark berry blue, and in the waves, a pale turquoise color leaps and bounces about while shades of cerulean blue sparkle and dance across the lake like watery Northern Lights and she is glad her newly streaked hair is now a waterfall blue. The ship glides through the surface of the lake like time itself, a horizontal clock measuring the minutes of their lives – smooth, steady, and simultaneously a slow lazy movement through water and an unfathomable race lurching through the confines of the lake toward a place where your life might flash before your eyes. Sarah swings her legs off the bed and sits carefully on the edge.

"Well now you have a view, Sarah," Morgan says, putting his arm around her. "Next we'll get you out of here. Back home."

"Where is my home, Morgan? You're always somewhere else. I don't think I have a home."

"You just hang up your hat and that's your home. I'll get you some hats."

She would like a new hat. Maybe their renovated house on Park Point will start to feel like her real home. She could get a hat rack. Sarah watches Morgan move the CD player. How handsome and strange he is, like a homeless movie star or a Nobel Prize winner who lives in an abandoned laboratory. He really doesn't fit into a category; he looks too scientific, too handsome, too messy, and then that air of health and excessive energy. Midway into the first act of *Tosca*, Sarah falls asleep.

---

TOM TROLL STANDS AT the doorway to Sarah's hospital room holding a stuffed seagull and a bouquet of daisies. The cloth partition around her bed is half open and through the beaded curtain, he can see that she is sound asleep. What to do. Should he announce himself and wake her up or should he just leave the seagull on the nightstand? He forgot about a vase for the flowers. Now what? He's never been good at these small dilemmas of life, and he's not sure if he's dressed up enough for the hospital with his tie and flannel shirt. He hadn't wanted to appear too formal, yet he feels odd, like he's forgotten something or he's doing something incorrectly.

Tom decides he'll wait a short while. He settles himself in the chair just out of view of Sarah so she won't feel she's being watched if she wakes up. Yet he shouldn't really sit so he can see the lake either. That would give the impression that he didn't care. He turns the chair so he can see neither Sarah nor the lake. He concentrates on the electrical outlets on the floor.

When Lilly comes to see Sarah, she finds Tom sitting patiently in a chair, with a seagull on his lap and holding a bouquet of daisies. Tom is startled and stands suddenly, dropping the flowers and nearly upsetting the chair. "I'm so foolish. I don't know what's the matter with me today," he whispers to Lilly and introduces himself. "I keep thinking how she was hit right there on Sixth Avenue in front of my shop. It makes me shake – look." He holds out his wavering hands and the seagull, which also appears to be trembling.

Lilly takes hold of the outstretched hand without the bird and holds it in her own. She begins to chant softly. Tom's hand becomes steady in Lilly's sure hands and her calm manner and soothing repetitious chant makes him feel almost at home in the hospital setting, even if she is wearing a gold sari and all that dangly jewelry.

"I never liked hospitals," he tells Lilly. "My mother died in this hospital. In the middle of the night. I didn't get there in time." He shakes his head slowly, obviously in pain, remembering the event. I knew she was gone – they called me at home and I rushed right down. I parked and ran to the emergency entrance and then hurried through the halls. It was so quiet, in the middle of the night like that. Hardly anyone in the hospital. Just long empty halls. I don't remember seeing anyone at all except the two nurses by her room. I kissed her forehead. I've always been glad I did that. Isn't that strange?"

Sarah watches her aunt and Tom through her beaded curtain. They are standing in the middle of the room holding hands with a seagull between them. She awoke to Lilly's chanting but maybe that was part of her dream. Now they are talking quietly. Is that seagull dead or alive? Is she dead or alive?

"Yoo hoo, Hello-oo," Lulu calls out nervously from the doorway, and Sarah starts to laugh but stops abruptly in pain.

MORGAN WALKS BAREFOOT in the sand of the peninsula. The water is icy cold as it washes over his feet. He can't figure out how she tracks him down. She should have been a spy or a private investigator, or maybe a lawyer. As soon as he walked into his room he knew it was Carmen. He heard the phone when he turned the key. He just knew. Concerned about Sarah. She had to know, she said. Wishing her dead probably.

Morgan stands still and looks out across the lake. How long has Carmen been following him? From how many countries? Across how many bodies of water? And calling from Finland now. No wonder he needs the jungle. All those women. Only Sarah and his native friends leave him alone, let him be himself, see past that Robert Redford thing, or whoever it is they're always reminded of.

He should have tried harder with Sarah. Let her get used to the jungle a little at a time. He was too abrupt in Peru when the mosquitoes were thick and then that unfortunate incident with the snake. If they had gone to a national park in this country, perhaps the Arches in Utah, yes, with the red rock bridges. He's always liked Utah. There's something spiritual about stone, especially at dusk when the rocks have a glow. Those curved arches of red rock, delicate as a dinosaur's neck or like an outdoor cathedral, a bare bones modern cathedral. Sarah would have liked the evening light on the red earth and stone. And they might have taken a boat down the Colorado to the grotto to hear the birds and their echoes in the stone amphitheater. Now they hold concerts there, formal classical concerts. What a place to hear Mozart – now that's something Sarah would have loved. And she would have felt peaceful, falling asleep under the stars after a good hike in that beautiful country, or after love under the Milky Way.

Would have. Would have. Why is he saying this? She'll get better. Of course. He speeds up, digging his heels into the sand. Why hasn't the doctor returned his call? He'll call from his room. He'll insist, have the doctor paged.

Funny though, Carmen finding him like that. If it weren't for Carmen he would still be in the jungle. She could always track him down, through Kila this time, and the embassy. What if Sarah had died? And smart Lilly Marlene, thinking to call the American Embassy. Morgan sits on a driftwood log and puts on his shoes. No sandpipers today. Probably too late and they've already gone south. Such strong, capable birds.

Morgan is happy to be at the new inn near the beach, but he liked the Radisson. He likes round buildings, and the Radisson's top floor with its revolving restaurant. You can eat your lunch while looking at the lake and rotating around the hills of Duluth. He'll ask Lilly to join him. He'll have a scotch, relax. Lilly can sip pineapple juice, served with one of those little umbrellas. They can watch the sunset over the lake and talk about Sarah. Lilly, with her mixture of Indian spirituality and Scandinavian practicality. It'll be good, watching the city lights come on, making plans. Somehow he is sure things are going to change. He is drawn to Sarah like when they first met. Funny, it's magnetic, actually magnetic. He feels it right in his bones. And her with her poor broken bones. Morgan sits in the parking lot by the beach contemplating his hands on the steering wheel.

---

SARAH STARES AT THE beaded curtain as if in a trance. The light makes each bead shine like a magic sphere, and the little globes of amber, corral, orange, red and gold, tinkle when she blows toward them. She knows it's night because it is perfectly quiet and dark except for the small night light Lilly left on for her, the one that makes the beads shine.

55

She doesn't recall actually walking to the window, only just being there, with the seagull on the window ledge. It was so clear to her and not at all like in a dream, unless it was one of those lucid dreams. How can one tell, with the pills they keep giving her. She doesn't know who spoke first. It seemed they had been talking like this forever and were simply resuming an old conversation.

"It's the moonlight I like," she said. "Down there on top of the water. I think I want to be there. Be part of the moonlight."

"It's nice, resting in the light. On the water like that. I do it all the time," said the seagull.

"I'm glad," Sarah said. "Perhaps you'll help me. I'd like that."

"Of course I'll help," said the seagull.

She stared at the moonlight on the lake in silence. As she walked back to the hospital bed she felt a ghost walk through her. It felt nice, like a soft wind. And then she was in bed and the stuffed seagull sat beside her water glass and she fell into a sleep as deep as death.

---

MORGAN HAD A BAD NIGHT. He slept, but fitfully so, restlessly. He was up several times during the night and finally decided he might as well get up. Now arriving at the hospital before the sun is up, there is just the first hint of dawn. Wearing a new blue shirt from the shop near the Radisson, he feels fresh and hopeful, and remembers to grab the Audubon magazine with the sandpiper on its cover from the back seat.

He hears the echo of his footsteps as he walks down the empty hallway. Sarah is asleep in her darkened room. He leans over her. Her eyes beneath the lids move wildly, jerkily, and her hair looks wet. He takes her hand in his and is shocked at its heat. Something is wrong. She doesn't wake when he speaks to her, nor when he gently lifts her hand. Her body is one barely perceptible shiver. He feels the shiver pass from her body to his.

A clammy chill tightens his throat and stiffens his walk as he rushes out into the hall to find help. At first he can't speak, and then the sounds come out of his mouth in little gulps of words. The nurse follows him. She calls the resident, who fortunately is on the same floor and just down the hall.

Morgan stands back while they examine her. He insists on knowing her temperature. It's 106. He sits down and listens to the young doctor explain how she is probably having a reaction to her pain medication. They'll run some tests, move her to intensive care, cool her down, and keep an eye on her.

# five

PULLING INTO THE DRIVEWAY, tired, and if not happy to be home, Stephen is at least relieved to be home. The garage smells of garbage. He missed his pickup day which was his own fault. He forgot to put it out the day before his trip, though he had planned the trip around garbage pickup day specifically to avoid this problem. Old smelly garbage is one thing he hates, truly hates. He has a sensitive nose.

He leaves his luggage in the hallway and takes the package to the kitchen and sets it down on the counter top. There are 26 messages on his answering machine. He listens to the first three: his backup garage door opener is ready; there's a new date from the guy who's to clean his gutters, chosen without consulting him. He snarls to himself. And one call from his travel agent. He knows there'll be a call from his publisher with some new trivial difficulty to deal with. Some new headache. No point in listening to the rest, not when he's tired. Enough for one day, it's late.

He walks from room to room, reclaiming his space, his house, his empty home. He flips through the mail. Bills, begging letters, a couple of catalogs. One letter, from his Aunt Ellie, in Ely. He sets the letter on top of the pile for morning. A little something to look forward to at tomorrow's breakfast. He spreads a dish cloth over the package on the counter and heads up the stairs and into his wife's office, still much the same as when she was alive.

He has that feeling that comes when he first enters the room, just for a moment, a fraction of a second – an awareness of Jeannie. It both pleases and depresses him, yet makes him feel a little renewed. Sometimes he tricks himself, allows himself to banish her to a long vacation, instead of death. Perhaps some little town in Portugal with pleasant narrow cobblestone streets, and window boxes filled with healthy pink geraniums. Yes, she could be a photographer in Portugal. She has a deadline, a book on Portuguese churches, particularly Portuguese church doors, entryways. Deadline. Wrong word, terrible word. He hates it, shakes his head.

In the hallway Stephen stares down at the narrow Persian carpet. This is where she walked barefoot with her pink toes and those rosy polished nails like rows of shiny flowers. On this very carpet. His own feet feel funny, kind of tingly inside his shoes and he wants to be barefoot right then – knows he'll forget or it just won't work later, never works later, when he's ready for bed and barefoot and steps out onto the hall carpet again. It'll be too late to get the feeling back. It only works in the moment the thought comes to him, like a little present. Later, even if he prepares carefully, retracing his path, his thoughts, it's forced and artificial. Just can't get it back.

There's something on the rug, some scrap of paper. He reaches down and picks it up. A sharp, horrid pain stabs the center of his hand. He's been stung by a wasp, a sneaky, half-dead wasp. Damn, damn it hurts like hell. In the dim light he couldn't see – didn't expect a wasp in the crinkled paper. What to do. Jeannie would know. Yes, he remembers. An antihistamine. Holding his hand by the wrist, he leads himself like an invalid to the bathroom.

By morning, Stephen's hand is swollen, red and painful. The pain is constant, like a continual shock in the center of his palm. He sits at the kitchen table and examines his hand under the magnifying glass he keeps beside the phone. No visible stinger. He vaguely recalls that only bees leave the stinger behind, not wasps or hornets. He'll ignore it; just refuse to give it a thought.

He enjoys his Aunt Ellie's newsy letter. Her handwriting is strikingly similar to his mother's hand. She always mentions how many deer she's seen in her yard. Sometimes she spots a moose. The bears are terrible, she writes. Into everyone's garbage, up in the apple trees. Her neighbor Flora's weeping birch split right in two when a bear sat on it. Stephen tries to picture this. He knows anything is possible up North. Over the years, he's made many visits to her house near the great forests of the Boundary Waters Canoe Area. Yes, from Duluth on up, anything is possible, which is precisely why he can do business with Hawk so easily. Buy a smoked fish, and five minutes later, make a deal on the shores of Gitche Gumee.

A cup of coffee is just what he needs, good and strong. He'll definitely visit his aunt at Christmas. He could use a piece of her home-made wild blueberry pie this morning. His own coffee is much better than his cousin's. Why Jim has to boil it to death, he does not understand. And then he refuses to grind the beans Stephen buys, even after he gave him that German coffee grinder last Christmas. If Stephen forgets to dump the unused coffee before he goes to bed, Jim reheats it in the morning. Boils it. He makes a good salary at the insurance company in Duluth so there's no reason for his stinginess. But then he's always been like that, even as a child he was miserly, telling Stephen each glass of water cost eleven cents. When he would let the water run so he could have a nice cold drink Jim would give him that eleven cents a glass line and look at him like he was a cad, like he had just killed a cat or something. Water waster, he'd tell Stephen. He can still hear him. "Stephen, that water is eleven cents a glass; you're pouring money straight down the drain." And he was just a kid, maybe nine years old, and acting like a fussy old man. Still, he lets Stephen use his car, which is much classier and newer than his own.

Recalling his cousin's idiosyncrasies, Stephen grins to himself, despite the wasp, and by the time he heads outside with the package under his arm he's in a jovial mood. "Eleven cents. Sure." In the garage the tools are in order, each in its place. Sometimes Jeannie made fun of his orderliness, as when he had wanted to make an index for his tools so he could keep track when someone borrowed an item, like when Fred borrowed the post hole digger and forgot who he borrowed it from. It made sense to Stephen, but Jeannie discouraged him and laughed gaily, telling him to wait until he was old to do that. She thought he was silly. He loved her laughter, rippling through the air like happiness itself, and the thought of her laughter makes him smile at the row of shovels hanging neatly on the garage wall.

*Her laughter, like a summer breeze.*

She didn't laugh at him. Never. She never made fun of him, just some of his ideas. But he did like an orderly life, and he had made a computer file for the tools anyway.

Several small orange pumpkins are scattered among the vines at the near end of the garden, still ripening under the fall sun. He'll leave them until later in the month. Otherwise, there's not much left, just the stubble from his one row of sweet corn, which was particularly good this year, though the peas and yellow beans also did well. All these years he had never before tried yellow beans, though he had always wanted to. Somehow he had categorized them as something he didn't plant and really for no particular reason, just a vague idea that the green beans were more reliable. Odd how a person gets these ideas about some minor thing like that. All these years he could have been enjoying yellow beans, he and Jeannie, they seemed more tender, and he liked the way they looked on a plate, so yellow and buttery.

A good recent rain has made the earth easy to dig, even in the field next to the last row of turnips.

"Hey Stephen, how you doing down there?" Fred calls out from his back yard as he strides across the gently sloping lawn. Stephen quickly replaces the earth where's he's started digging and kicks some dried weeds over the fresh hole. He moves nonchalantly to the turnip row and digs out a couple of purple and white turnips by the time Fred gets to the garden, holds them up for his inspection.

"Nice work. What are they, parsnips?'

"Turnips. Want some?"

"Nah. I don't care for those root things, except for potatoes. Too bitter. My favorite vegetable is ice cream." Fred laughs at his own joke and Stephen attempts a laugh, but it comes out fake. Realizing that Fred won't know the difference, he ends up laughing easily, naturally.

"Come on, I want to show you something," Stephen says, walking toward the garage and away from the package he's left not too well hidden beside the rock that marks his digging place in the field. Think quick, what can he show Fred in the garage. He doesn't want to invite him inside the house; he'd stay forever. That new fishing pole, he's never seen that. Actually it isn't new, but he's never used the thing since he let his fishing days slip away.

"Oh that's real nice, Stephen," Fred pulls out the line and reels it in. "Smooth. Top quality."

After Fred leaves he retrieves the package, slips it into a plastic bag and leans it up in the back of the hall closet, prepared to wait until dark before heading back to the garden. The day flies by, taken up with various domestic errands. Calls, short trips about town, to the laundry, the library. At precisely 6:30 p.m., Fred's truck pulls out of the drive, heading for the monthly meeting of the Scarlet Maple Writer's Club. Stephen had been quite surprised when he first heard that Fred liked to

write, and then Fred invited him to come as his guest at one of
their monthly meetings. That was over two years ago, one of
the first outings after Jeannie died.

There were about ten regulars in the group, including Fred.
They met in the basement of the telephone building in a
rectangular meeting room not much larger than the table they
sat around. A neighbor he doesn't really know, except to wave
at when he's out for a run, impressed him the most. She read her
poem about how a large metropolitan area consists of little
neighborhoods that are like friendly villages of people. It was a
good poem. Actually a very good poem and he still doesn't know
her name, even though they live in the same "village." It was an
unusual name which he couldn't quite catch. It sounded like Laura
Lee, or Laura Dee. Maybe it was her accent, which seemed
slightly French. He could find out. Just stop and visit, when he's
out running. She's often out in her front yard flower beds.

It was a fine group of people really. The first person to read
was a young woman dressed in white, whom he nicknamed
Snow White. She read the first chapter of her work-in-progress.
It was about eating breakfast and he remembers a part about
oatmeal and a child who had to eat cold lumpy oatmeal before
she could leave the kitchen table and go off to school. The
child dreaded the oatmeal as much as she dreaded being late for
school and how it was a dilemma she faced every morning.

They went around the table, each person taking a turn
reading from their recent writing. When Fred's turn came
around, he read the minutes from his last Kiwanis Club
meeting. At first Stephen thought it was a joke, and had leaned
forward smiling. No joke though. This was Fred's regular
contribution to their monthly meeting and what he always read.

For his own turn, Stephen read a couple of pages from his
last book – a section on the Penitentes of New Mexico and
their crucifixion ritual. The group paid equal attention to
everyone's writing, whether poetry, Kiwanis Club minutes or

the crosses people bear. It was enjoyable actually, having that undivided attention given to his work. Of course he never read his own work to his students, and a person rarely gets an opportunity to read out loud as an adult. Yes, he liked it, and remembers how sweaty his hands got as he read about the man portraying Christ. He had called out in sorrow because they were using rope to tie him to the cross, instead of stakes. The actor had considered it shameful to have it so easy, after they gave up the use of stakes following a death and considerable negative publicity.

Stephen would have gone back if it hadn't been for the smoking. Every person in town who smoked must have belonged to that writers group. He was the only non-smoker at the table. The saving grace was that only one person could smoke at a time; otherwise their smoking would set off the fire alarm, which apparently it had done at one of their first meetings. When Snow White finished her cigarette, Fred lit up, and when Fred finished, Laura Lee, Dee, would light up, and so on around the table and back to the beginning, skipping only Stephen.

The minute he got home he threw all of his clothing into the wash and stepped into the shower. Even his billfold smelled of smoke. From then on he has referred to Fred's writing group as the SSS, for Stinking Smoking Scribblers, which was a little cruel, but made for a handy notation on his calendar. And were the Kiwanis Club members aware that their secretary regularly shared their activities with non-members? Fred read the minutes well, with studied expression, as though he were reading lines from a well-known play, Shakespeare even. He could tell Fred put a lot of thought and effort into the minutes, both the writing and the reading. Probably he read them aloud to himself several times, as a kind of rehearsal before meetings. Stephen imagines him pacing back and forth in his living room reciting the lines. "A resolution was passed unanimously, to make an annual contribution of money and winter coats to the

South Dakota Rosebud Reservation, located in the heart of the historic Wounded Knee territory." A good line, easy to remember, and a good cause.

In the garden, it was easier than he thought to find the spot again and scrape aside the weeds and rubble he had spread over the loose earth. His earlier probing with the shovel had hit the box buried below and he knew if he worked carefully and steadily he would finish quickly. He digs through the rich loose soil, shoveling the dirt onto a pile at the garden's edge. Although the night is dark, Stephen's eyes adjust well and he ignores the unearthed night crawlers, writhing in their slick pink skin under the moonlight. The smell of the earth is what he notices most as he continues digging, and how it is both repellent and pleasant, almost compelling Stephen to breathe deeply, to acknowledge the earth, to relish its lovely horror. It seems too late in the year for fireflies, but there they are, flickering beside him and out over the field like low-lying stars. Stars above, stars below. If he were a poet he would use that line. Laura Lee could write a poem about fireflies and stars. Surprised at his dreaminess in the middle of his digging, he shovels faster until the top of the box is completely uncovered. He kneels and slides his hand over the box and along the short end, feeling his way toward the handle. Slowly and carefully, he drags the box up and out of the earth.

# six

SARAH'S CONDITION HAS STABILIZED and both Lilly and Morgan are keeping vigil in her room. Lilly is awake but resting quietly with her eyes closed and her hands folded in her lap, oblivious to the silk scarf that has fallen across one side of her face. Sarah's temperature has returned to normal and her tests revealed nothing unusual. Still, Morgan could tell the young resident monitoring Sarah was simply guessing when he listed possible causes for her earlier high temperature and near seizure in ER.

Morgan enjoyed his share of the yogurt drink Lilly brought for Sarah, for its cooling properties and good flavor, and it was heartening to see her sip the lassi through a straw with such relish. Afterwards, she fell asleep with a slight smile on her lips, as though she were in the middle of a good dream. Morgan chews on a mint leaf from his drink and moves closer to Sarah's bed. Her hair is matted against her scalp but she looks beautiful. The rosiness of her cheeks makes him think of a wild rose, the kind she tells him not to pick because the petals drop as soon as they're picked. Still, she looks so soft, so … he can't find a word.

Lilly opens her eyes and is pleased to see Morgan focused so intently on Sarah and absent-mindedly caressing her sheet. She closes her eyes again and this time dozes off. Not until 2:00 a.m. do Lilly and Morgan leave the hospital, yawning their goodnights, both sleepy and hopeful. Morgan heads toward his hotel on Park Point and Lilly drives up the avenue to High Street.

AS SOON AS LILLY TURNS into the driveway she sees a light in her backyard. Entering by the front door, she walks through the semi-dark living room to the kitchen where she looks out onto the backyard and waits for her eyes to adjust. The grass looks green and neat, thanks to Sarah's earlier raking. The white marble bird bath by the old birch tree glows under the light of the moon. The only sound is the slow rhythmic chirping of a single cricket. Lilly waits and watches for movement. Though she hasn't smelled skunk since early summer, that's what she suspects has set off the motion detector. She has a comfortable easiness throughout her body, now that Sarah is better. Her feet feel warm and heavily anchored to the floor, but in a tottery sort of way, like one of those life-sized cartoon character punching balloons with weights in the bottom. Not the slightest breeze blows in the yard.

Morgan was his old self tonight, so caring, much as he was when he and Sarah were first married. He'll take good care of Sarah. Lilly had considered delaying her trip to Delhi, canceling her flight, but is now optimistic and looking forward to seeing her son in India. He did well managing his father's business after Ravi's death. "Devi, my dear Devi," she says softly to herself. Still she's glad he sold the business. She's happy for his wonderful gift for making music, for his life as a musician.

Still standing at the window, she catches herself slipping into sleep, then steadies herself and through fluttering eyelids sees the outline of a large bear beneath the apple tree to the left of the birch. She tiptoes to the backdoor to make sure she locked the door, not that bears can unlock doors, but they do sometimes get in through screens. The door is unlocked, and slightly ajar. Now totally alert, she locks the door quickly and as quietly as she can, and is as aware of the dark basement stairs behind her as of the bear outside. Taking a deep breath, she turns on the basement light and walks down the stairs.

Nothing. No one. Her new indigo sari is still soaking in a pan in the wash basin. She left so quickly after Morgan called. Rinsing the sari, she admires the color, the deep dark blue of night, and momentarily forgets about Sarah and Morgan and even about the bear. After spreading the cloth over the wooden rungs of the clothes rack, she looks in the fruit cellar, just to be sure, just to check it out.

Nothing unusual here. She has always loved this room with its neat wooden shelves lined with jars of jams, jellies and preserves, bight and clear as jewels under the bare light bulb. There are glass jars of red current jelly, sparkling raspberry and strawberry jams, blueberry sauce the color of her sari, plus peaches and apricots, round as golden suns. On the top shelf there are still three jars of her sister's pickles, labeled in her own handwriting. She used to eat one jar a year, but now she just looks at the jars as friendly reminders of Lilah's years on the earth.

Back upstairs at the kitchen window she notes the bear still nosing around under the apple tree. She really doesn't mind; it's just fattening up for hibernation, though last year she was angry when a mother bear and her cub ruined the gooseberry bushes. She had just come into the house with an armload of rhubarb and knew the bears must have been watching her when she tossed the leaves onto the compost heap. They devoured the gooseberries as she stood watching. No gooseberry pie that year. Oh well.

Leaving the bear to its apples, she retrieves the mail and finds a note from Lulu.

*Dear Lilly,*
*I hope Sarah is better – let me know when you get home.*

Well, too late to call Lulu tonight. She'll call in the morning. Lilly smiles, knowing Lulu would want to race right up and have a bear-watching party with popcorn, if she were to call her now.

## Konnie Ellis

*I met a man at the Farmer's market this morning, between the rutabagas and the carrots. He's the caretaker up at Chester Park. Real friendly person. Invited me to go fishing.*

*Lulu.*

*P.S. He plays the accordion.*

# seven

WITH FIREFLIES FLICKERING over Stephen's garden, he kneels over the box at the edge of the field and methodically brushes dirt off its top with a whisk broom. He swipes the surface clean with an old rag, glances over his shoulder, checking for lights or someone out walking their dog, then takes the key out of his pocket and opens the lock. The click of the lock affects him like an unlocking in his very bones. Just as he is about to raise the lid, he hears a rustling in the grass, and though startled, he turns his head slowly. What would he say if someone has been watching, spying on him all this time? But it's only a rabbit at the end of the turnip row. Its ears are erect, giving it a worried look, as if questioning the propriety of the scene before him.

There she is, lying at the bottom of the box. The wooden Madonna looks smaller than he remembered. Her beatific smile calms him as he lifts her out and places her gently on the beach towel. There are no signs of moisture having seeped into the box. No dirt, no bugs. The gold leaf trim on the child's garment is dazzling under the night sky. He touches the grain of the wood curving over her cheek bones before rolling the statue up in the blue towel which is the same color as the Madonna's robe, what's left of it, which is just bits of color here and there on the wood, though there are large patches of darker blue on her head covering.

Stephen has not allowed himself to unwrap the new sculpture until now, keeping to his little self-imposed ritual, and thus he had only seen it briefly when he was on the boat when Hawk took it out of its crate. He has gone over the scene on the boat several times, concentrating on the details so he would be able to recall the saintly face clearly at will. He especially remembers the eyes as Hawk lifted her out of the sawdust and how she had seemed almost ready to blink or smile for him that evening on the lake.

Hawk had stood there holding the statue of Mary and the child, breathing in that asthmatic way of his, ruminating and spitting into a spittoon. He wore a black sweatshirt torn off at the elbows, greasy jeans, and lumberjack boots. His right forearm was covered with what looked like greenish black lichen, and unlike the other arm, had no hair. Stephen had tried not to stare. His lips were stained a reddish brown, with a bulge on one side of his mouth which swelled as he puckered and sloshed tobacco, yet he seemed more upbeat than the last time. Maybe. He was hard to read. Above them was a mobile made from Copenhagen snuff boxes and covers that dangled from fish line and turned slowly in the sea breeze. The scene was not normal. But neither was his business there, the procurement of a black market Madonna, probably, and of course, the drugs. Hawk wrapped the statue in *The Winnipeg Sun*, and tucked the other package into its flap.

Stephen remembers the sick feeling he had as he climbed the ladder to the deck of the boat with the statue tucked under his arm. Hawk was right behind him and he could hear the waves slapping against the side of the boat. Even though he had been anxious to get going he had asked Hawk if he could get him another one, next time. One with more gold. He hadn't been able to help himself. Hawk had told him to call him at Christmas. "That'll cost you more. More gold, more money." That phrase had stood out.

Stephen finds he's talking to himself. "More gold, more money," he mumbles, remembering. The rabbit is still there, nibbling on a turnip top, its fur glittery under the moonlight. Hawk's words seem to linger over the field, what he said before pulling away in the boat: "Godspeed, Stephen." And then Hawk's sharp laugh stayed with him like a shadow as he walked along the shore until the only sound was that of the boat motor before Stephen climbed back up to the road.

*His laughter, like polluted water.*

Stephen's hands are shaking as he places the new Mary and child into the box. He replaces the lock, lowers the box, and quickly shovels dirt into place, stomping over the earth in as respectful a manner as he can manage. Although the evening is cool, he feels sweat run into his eyes.

From behind the darkened garage, Fred watches Stephen's macabre night digging in the garden. He feels his heart beat wildly in his chest while he watches Stephen scatter grass and leaves over the earth. Fred rushes off down the street toward where he has parked his car, sure that he's been right all along, he knew, he just knew something wasn't right with Stephen.

Hanging up the shovel in the garage, Stephen's hands have stopped shaking and that sneaky feeling of joy floods through him, something he first experienced as a child, walking home with a stolen candy bar in his pocket. Eating it alone in his room, it was better than other candy bars. Much better.

Stephen has finished his coded entries and is just shutting down his computer when he spots Fred's car lights turning into his driveway down the street. Well pleased with his timing, he picks up his freshly unearthed Madonna from the kitchen table and a couple of Reese's peanut butter cups, and heads down the stairs to the basement.

This is his third Mary. He knows he should pay more attention to the child, but he's not ready for that. He can't help but focus on Mary, his beautiful Mary. He removes his shoes, dons his old brown hooded bathrobe with its rope belt and pulls the hood over his head as he opens the door to the old coal bin which he has transformed into a sound-proof music room with speakers in each corner. He sets a candle on a worn piece of red velvet cloth on a log set on end in the center of the room. Beginning his Latin prayer, he lights the candle and sets the icon into its niche in the wall, and locking the door behind him, turns the Gregorian chant up full blast.

# eight

LILLY HAS CLEANED the house in preparation for Sarah's homecoming, and the arrival of Sam Light, the yogi Morgan arranged as a guide for Sarah's recuperation. The rooms have been freshened with sage. Last night Lilly walked the perimeter of each room with a home-made sage smudge, and the air still hints of a slightly burnt and medicinal scent. She spots Lulu turning into the driveway, as usual, her upper wheels cut across the front lawn before bumping back onto the driveway.

Lulu bustles in with an armload of rhubarb. "Hmmm. Smells nice. Interesting." Her own house smells of cooked cabbage, and cats, she's sure. So she's been told, but she's used to it. "Notice anything new?" she says, tapping the pin on her lapel. "It's a present from Leif," Lulu explains, running a finger over the pin. Lilly thinks it's a willow leaf, or a citrus leaf of some kind. She's curious about this new friend, Leif, who volunteered to pick up Sam Light at the airport today, so she'll meet him soon enough.

Lilly is truly happy about Sarah's coming home, especially with Morgan's enthusiasm for making everything right and comfortable for Sarah. He bought a set of extra soft bamboo sheets, candles, and fruit. Plus some bird books, and a coffee table book on butterflies. And mainly, he's actually here. "Are you sure Leif will be able to find Morgan's yogi all right at the airport, Lulu?"

She says Leif made a little sign he's going to hold up, like his sister-in-law told him they do in Minneapolis. She says Leif's a good smooth driver, and if he gets off on the edge of the road, he gets right back on. "I don't even have to tell him," Lulu says.

They have tea in the living room while they wait. The Jasmine tea is relaxing and they both feel peaceful, with hope in their hearts. Lilly and Lulu are both in their 50s, and as solid as the rocks along Lake Superior's North Shore, and at the same time, both are fragile as flowers. Lulu is the lilac, and Lilly the orchid, exotic in a blue sari and delicate silk scarves flowing over her shoulders like pale purple waterfalls. Lilly wears earrings and necklaces of such fine gold that they appear like strands of sun reflected in water. Lulu is substantial in a navy blue pants suit and green blouse with large multi-colored flowers, and her new orange lapel pin.

"Leif gave me this pin last Saturday after he showed me his gun collection."

Lilly bluntly states that she doesn't like guns, that they are made for killing. She's seriously concerned that her dear friend is getting close to someone who'll be trouble. Lulu insists he never shoots animals, or rarely, and trying to make up for the gun collection, mentions how well he plays the accordion. She tells how he shoots clay pigeons and that she had the best day with Leif, watching him shoot – the best day since seeing the bear in Leif Erickson Park.

"That was a good day," Lilly agrees, hoping the bear did all right. Poor thing. "Sarah's dad shot clay pigeons. They used some kind of hand thrower to fling them into the air. He was quite an expert, Sarah's dad. Quite the sharp shooter. Even won a marksmanship award."

"Is that right? Well, how about that," Lulu says, genuinely surprised. She says Leif used to use black and yellow clay pigeons, but now they use brighter colors. He uses mostly orange. And some lime green ones that are a glow-in-the-dark color and they burst into bright colored balls of dust when they're hit, like fireworks. Lulu likes the orange ones, like little suns exploding in the sky. Next time she's going to give it a try. "No reason I shouldn't be able to shoot," she half asks, half states.

Lilly had been both fascinated and horrified, watching Sarah's dad slip black and yellow disks high into the sky, breaking each with a single shot before the pieces fell to the earth. Both the pitching and the shooting were rhythmic and exact, and she recalls the hypnotic effect it had on her at the time, watching him shoot like that at the Gun Club up by Trap Woods. Now there are homes all over where the woods used to be. She understands how Lulu liked watching Leif shoot, yet wishes she didn't.

She sets her tea cup aside and begins to chant. She chants for the bear and for Lulu, for her son in India, and for Sarah, and for the happiness of all living things.

———————

SARAH IS THE FIRST TO ARRIVE. Morgan helps her up the steps, one careful step at a time. Her Norwegian sweater is draped over her shoulders, and she wears her new metal and white leather back brace over a black turtle neck which creates an unintentional skeletal effect. As soon as they step inside, Leif Larson and Sam Light turn down the hill and Leif cuts across the grass, bouncing back onto the driveway, a la Lulu. As sometimes happens, everyone arrives within minutes of one another. Jessie, with her lavender hair and tattooed husband, Rolf, arrive with flowers, followed by Tom Troll carrying a stuffed mallard duck. Gigi and Jeep come with a basket of fruit, and Julia follows, a bottle of champagne tucked under her arm.

After everyone meets and greets one another and Sarah is settled onto the chaise longue next to the piano, Gigi asks Julia to sing the recipe song, "to make everyone feel at home," she says. Leif offers to accompany on his "squeeze box," and, without waiting to hear if Julia wants an accompanist, he dashes out the door to retrieve the accordion from his car. Morgan sits at the piano and strikes a single note while looking expectantly up at Julia. She explains that the tune is Oh Holy Night, and the words she will sing are the recipe for a traditional hot dish and you can substitute tofu if you're a vegetarian.

Morgan knows the song, but only knows the words in French. He is perfectly comfortable with an October Christmas carol with recipe lyrics. Leif's accordion looks like it weighs more than he does, but he slings its straps over his wiry shoulder easily and stands in readiness next to Julia. She sings like an angel from Florence newly freed from a fresco, and her voice is both holy and hungry "…a pinch of nut-meg…."

The song is pure and lovely, weird and happy, and seems to express the essence and heart of northern Minnesota. Leif is tearful by the time they finish, and Sarah is laughing and crying from the pain in her back. Leif says it was the onion, the line about the onion that made him cry, which makes Sarah laugh all the more, holding her stomach in agony. Morgan rushes over to comfort her, and Sarah notices Gigi eyeing her handsome husband like a lioness considering dinner.

After Sarah takes a Percocet and settles back onto her chaise longue, Leif plays a song he learned from his grandfather called "The Old Woods" song, a haunting folk melody from the old country. Knowing how sad it can make people, as soon as he finishes, he starts into a lively version of "Roll out the Barrel," tapping his foot and jerking his shoulders and head in funny little energetic beats. Sam Light surprises everyone by asking Lulu to polka, and Lilly cajoles Tom into joining her for the dance. Jessie and Rolf make the polka look like a cool new dance, and Julia dances by herself, happy and lovely in the doorway. Gigi and Jeep slow dance to the polka, and Morgan bounces Sarah's hand until he notices that she has fallen asleep.

The welcome party is short and sweet. After Sarah falls asleep Lilly passes around copper glasses of freshly made chai, a wooden bowl of pistachios, rutabaga puffs and lefse triangles with goat cheese and cloudberry jam. The conversation is quiet and almost secretive while Sarah sleeps. Sam talks about his upcoming weekend enlightenment workshop in Minneapolis and how beautiful he finds Duluth. He is staying on Park Point in a home on the beach which Lulu says must be a block from the senior center where the Buoys and Gulls meet. She had signed up to join the Buoys and Gulls on their fall leaf bus trip up the shore, but now she's cancelled since Leif doesn't like bus trips or old people, she tells everyone. Leif explains how being old has nothing to do with one's age, and says his seventy-three years have nothing to do with his "real " age, and Lilly compliments him on this insight. Jeep keeps looking at his watch and Gigi tries to involve Morgan in conversation but he is distracted and in his own world as he watches over Sarah and sips his chai. He begins to hum a Brazilian lullaby, and Lilly spreads an Indian coverlet over Sarah. Jessie hands Morgan a bottle of sparkling blue nail polish for Sarah.

"Thanks for coming. It's been lovely," Lilly tells the group as she walks them to the door. "Do come again."

From the driveway Lulu calls out, thanking Lilly for the chokecherry jam she gave her in exchange for the rhubarb.

"We're going over to Superior," Lulu adds. "To see the neurotic dancers."

"Exotic. Exotic dancers," Leif bellows out, in his high shrill voice. "Belly dancers."

Lilly smiles to herself as they drive away; hopeful for the best, hopeful that Leif's enthusiasms are not misguided. Picking up empty cups, she considers asking Tom Troll for dinner some evening. Perhaps after she returns from India. She sets the gull on a low table where the mallard rests, one bird beside the brass Buddha and the other behind the plastic Mary she recently found at a garage sale. The Buddha holds a shiny gold cross, and is garlanded with some of the last marigolds of the year. A vase with a single bright maple branch finishes the still life. The red maple leaves are still crisp and Lilly is pleased, knowing her dearly departed Lutheran minister friend, Bjarne Johnson, would be content with the scene. It was Bjarne who welded the cross onto the Buddha's hand. He ordered it from the Missouri Synod catalog and taught himself how to weld, being a serious handyman and a good one too. She knows that if he were still around he would fix that door bell.

"Oh Morgan. It's so good to have her home from the hospital. So good. You know, she's changed. And you have too," Lilly says.

"I know, I know. All I can think is the years we've wasted. What happens to people? Why are we so foolish? Well, I should speak for myself, certainly not you. Morgan rolls the bottle of blue nail polish around in the palm of his hand before setting it down beside his empty chai glass.

"Perhaps Sam Light will enlighten us all. What do you think of him, so far?"

"I'm trying to keep an open mind, but he reminds me of someone I knew – this chief's son who stole a pig. He has the same sneaky eyes. I don't like his smile either. He is polite, certainly, and neat with his white clothing. He grew up in Brooklyn. His credentials looked good, but now I'm not so sure. I remember that pig. It had a black spot over its eye, like a dog," Morgan says, and abruptly claps his hands, unintentionally waking Sarah.

"Oh, they're gone. I'm in a dream," Sarah says, shifting her body carefully to lie on her opposite side, and without looking at either Morgan or Lilly, describes her dream and how she was at a party or a lecture, just sitting on a chair waiting for some event to begin, and she and a nice young man sat together and talked. He seemed to like her but she thought he was too young to look at her the way he was looking at her, but they could still be friends, she didn't mind. It was comfortable how they just knew each other without even talking, like they were old friends, and then before she knew it they were at her house, and she was in the bathroom, and he was just outside the door and she knew he was dangerous. Yet she opened the door, and now he wasn't young, and a voice said it didn't last long, that madness, and he said it only lasts half an hour, at most. But she could see from his eyes that he was crazy and that he was a monster and his eyes had been sewn up and then reopened and she saw where the stitches had been. Then he was gone and she was falling down the stairs and underwater plants and anemones with long iridescent tentacles were tumbling after her and she knew they were harmless, even though they were green and blue. But then the scary thing appeared, and it was so strong and violent that she was lucky to get it back into its jar and screw the cover on tight. Sarah holds Morgan's hand tight, to make the nightmare go away. He smoothes her hair and wipes away a tear until she calms down and falls back to sleep.

"It's the pills," Morgan says.

"Her spirit is struggling," Lilly adds.

Morgan and Lilly watch Sarah sleep until the phone rings. Lilly answers the phone in the kitchen, and Morgan is right behind her. She hands the phone to Morgan.

"You can't be here," Morgan says, horrified that Carmen is calling him here from the Duluth Radisson.

"I'm having baked brie with blueberries," she tells him. "I'm in the revolving restaurant. The blueberries are still warm. So good. They serve the brie in little puff balls on top of these warm mounds of blueberries. Six, I think. Six little brie things, that is. I ate them while I watched a boat go under the bridge. The bridge goes up and then the boat goes through and then the bridge comes down and then the cars go over the bridge. The cars have to wait for the bridge to go up and then they have to sit there while the boat goes through and they can't drive across until the bridge comes down again. The bridge is part of the road."

"Now we're turning toward the city," Carmen continues. "I can see all the bright leaves on the trees and the roof tops and the lights of the town are coming on. There are red lights on three radio towers. Let's see, there are thirteen towers altogether. There's another one. It just turned red. That makes four with red lights."

"You can't be talking to me. Not here," Morgan says in an angry quiet tone. He hangs up the phone. It immediately rings again. He picks it up, knowing it's useless to pretend he's not there. "Yes, I'll call you," he says, as quietly as he can, hoping Lilly won't overhear.

Morgan is looking out the window toward the creek when Lilly sets two small glasses on the table. From far back in a corner cupboard she retrieves an unopened bottle of Apricot Brandy. Morgan has never known Lilly to drink spirits.

"We need to talk," Lilly says as she fills the glasses.

———————

THE NEXT MORNING, Sarah wakes early, and for one brief beautiful moment, she is herself and at one with the peaceful morning. The moment passes and she wakes to the reality of her first day out of the hospital and rolls to one side to push herself upright. Slowly she swings her legs over the side of the bed as instructed by the physical therapist. Her brace is propped beside a pillow and she can just reach its strap to pull it to her. She wraps it around her chest and holds her breath, pulling the metal latch into place. She is not to get up without wearing the brace. There are so many rules to follow, so many instructions.

Taking tiny steps, she works her way toward the kitchen, pausing in the hallway to steady herself. This is the strangest part of the house since Lilly removed all the doors leading to the rooms, except for the one bedroom door. She replaced the other seven doors with beaded curtains, which tinkle as a person walks down the hall. Somehow the sound is different now, with her slow baby steps. The sounds of the glass beads reminds her of last spring at the edge of Cherry Lake, where the ice had broken into thin glassy fractures that clinked against one another creating a music like a Takemitsu quartet.

How strange it feels to be part brace. Is she awake? She feels goofy. Could she be turning into a new form of beetle, with a metal and white leather brace, some new creation from a Kafka story? Sarah glides through the last beaded curtain into the living room, caressed by the cold bright beads which ripple over her brace like a xylophone. Following her feet to the kitchen she is surprised to see it's snowing. Big white flakes of snow are falling over the yard, thousands of flakes changing the landscape, softening the air, falling like a curtain of atoms, of matter. Morgan once described all matter as moving simultaneously within itself. Could a person's molecules rearrange themselves and fall like snow, reorganized into something new, someone new, a snowman, a snow horse?

Feeling cleansed by watching the snow, Sarah decides to take a shower. She'll do it by herself before anyone gets up. She'll be careful. Maybe even wash her hair which feels greasy and stringy. Carefully. Don't wake Lilly, or Morgan. Don't bend. Don't trip. Hold the wall along the way. Small precise steps.

The doctor said it was okay. She could shower, or even take a bath without the brace, as long as she keeps her spine absolutely straight. She hangs her flannel nightgown on the bathroom door knob and unhooks the brace. Careful now, one step at a time and into the tub. First, how to turn on the water. Kneel down, back straight, reach out, back straight, reach, reach. There, now turn the knob. Sarah looks at the nice warm water gushing out as though she's never encountered indoor plumbing before. Add bubble bath. Lots of bubbles. So fresh and warm. Don't stay long. Mustn't slip. Wash your hair. You'll need to stand. Easy does it, up under the shower. Still a little banana shampoo left. Not able to bend, shampoo in one hand, she stands straight as a rod as the water pours over her hair and face. The shampoo drizzles down over her cheeks and her eyes until the water runs clear. Done. Clean. Now, with wet hair, so vulnerable and pale, and dripping all over the floor, she slips on the dry nightgown, nicely warmed from the heater below the towel rack. She clicks herself back into the refuge of the metal brace. She did it, and all by herself.

Sarah sits stiffly at the edge of the couch drying her hair. She feels oddly safe within the shell of her brace inside the noisy silence and smiles to herself under the drone of the dryer, considering what sort of beetle she might become. Perhaps a ladybug, sitting on a leaf on a summer's day, or a firefly with iridescent lights flickering across an evening field of wild flowers. And just where are the ladybugs and fireflies in winter? She is considering how it would be to become a winter beetle, here in Duluth, a magical white artic beetle, when Morgan stands before her smiling and saying something which she can't hear and without the sound of his voice she notices how much older he looks this morning. She turns the dryer onto high instead of off by mistake. By the time she is finished with her hair, she hears the sound of the car driving away.

"I don't know what it is, Aunt Lilly, and I care very much about Morgan, but on the other hand I feel so detached. Mostly I'm just hungry for breakfast. My reactions are off. I don't know what's wrong with me," she says, heading toward the kitchen.

"We'll just have breakfast and watch it snow."

"I feel like I'm changing channels on TV, and just clicking to a more normal scene, away from some tragedy."

"So you showered by yourself this morning, and washed your hair, I see."

"I did," she says. Sarah runs her fingers along the swatch of blue hair, noticing the texture, how it's different, thicker, than her own finer, silkier hair. Aware that she has maneuvered herself into the kitchen chair like an old person, she is grateful for her aunt's tact, even as she pours their morning tea.

Watching the snow fall over the backyard, Sarah remembers the bird she heard out in the garden back in June. She could hear the bird's frantic cries, yet she didn't go into that part of the garden, not wanting to see a wounded bird in its final distress. Then back in the house she had forgotten about the bird until the weekend. When she was picking strawberries for breakfast, she remembered and looked through the tall grass and bushes until she found the dead bird on the ground. It was a young starling with a black string twisted around its leg, the string hanging from a branch of a honeysuckle bush. She could easily have freed the bird from the string, if only she had looked, investigated. Basically she had killed the bird.

"So sad, Sarah, on such a beautiful day?" "The snow is beautiful," Lilly sighs. All the suffering, all the beauty. Lilly pats Sarah's hand and they both pick up their teacups and sip in unison.

---

LULU IS PEELING AN APPLE when she sees Lilly on TV with the protesters at Spirit Mountain. Lilly is holding a sign and singing that humming kind of singing she does, and there are drums too. Lilly's sign says "Save Spirit Mountain Forest." Lulu puts on her glasses so she can read the other signs. She sees one that says "Leave the Spirits in Peace," and another that reads "No Condos on Grandma's Grave." There are Indians with long hair, Lilly calls them something else, indigenous. Yes, that's it, or close. And Lulu knows it's important to use the right words. Lilly's Devi lives in India, the real India, and here we have Native Americans, Lulu says to herself, using Lilly's assured inflection, like a good teacher, a nice teacher. Much like Miss Massey, back in first grade. She wishes she were better with words; she's just never been good with words. Such nice hair. She likes the braids. Too bad so many have a problem with alcohol. That's a spirit problem too. Strong spirits. She'll have to talk to Lilly about that; she always feels better when she talks to Lilly about things that seem bad or impossible.

The apple peel comes off in one long curl. She is on the next apple when she spots Morgan. He's holding a sign too, but it's too small to read and he's turned to the side. A woman with red hair is standing close to him, touching his arm. Too close. Lulu knows trouble when she sees it. She hasn't watched soap operas all these years for nothing.

The protest coverage breaks for a Daugherty Hardware commercial about washing machines. Lulu liked their old ad better, the one with the lady who says "And *no* whining." "And no whining," Lulu echoes to her apple as she chops it into pie pieces. Good thing Lilly doesn't have a TV. Now what would Sarah think if she saw that? Morgan and that redhead. Oh my, is she all by herself while they are all out protesting? She'd better get right up there. She can be back by the time the pie is done. Lulu quickly tucks the top crust into place and slides the pie into the oven.

Lulu finds Sam Light standing on the porch ringing the doorbell when she arrives.

"Well Good Morning," Sam says brightly. "Lulu, isn't it?"

"Yes, hello. It's out of order," she says as she bustles across the lawn. "They're not home. You wait here and I'll go around back."

Lulu lets herself in the backdoor, and finds Sarah dozing in the back bedroom, an open book on her lap. She opens her eyes when Lulu greets her.

"You look pretty, Sarah," Lulu tells her.

"Oh, Lulu," Sarah says, opening her eyes half way. "Morning."

"And Good Morning to you. Where's Lilly and Morgan?" Lulu asks, to see if Sarah knows.

"Spirit Mountain. Protesting. So they won't cut down the trees to build condos. It's a sacred forest. They made signs last night." Sarah smiles to herself over Morgan's sign, which was way too small and with far too many words. He listed all the major birds and mammals from the area, plus phone and web sites for several environmental and Native American sites, as if anyone other than Morgan could remember entire lists of website addresses. She feels herself at the edge, ready to drift off, now quite against her wishes. She had wanted to write "This is *our* tropical forest," but wasn't sure if that made sense; the pills made her so crazy and uncertain.

"Lulu, I'm falling asleep. Afraid I'm not very good company. I took a pain pill and it's pulling me into sleep. Did Lilly tell you about her new phone, one of those picture phones so you can see who's calling? Well, not quite a phone. We could see Morgan on Park Point. Oh, I'm so tired."

Lulu watches Sarah sleep for a few moments, then remembers Sam at the door. She'll check the phone with the pictures next time. You'd think she'd get that doorbell fixed before getting a phone like that. Sam mustn't come in. She'll just tell him to go away. Morgan probably means well, but Sarah is in no condition for her yoga, for this yogi expert. Anyway, she'll tell him to always call first. He should know that, if he's supposed to be so enlightened. Lulu pats her hair, thinking how she'll need to comb her hair and not call on the new phone when she's still in her bathrobe. She's surprised Lilly would get such a new-fangled phone.

Driving home, Lulu realizes she was a bit short with Sam, sending him away like that. Almost scolding him, in fact, but she was just remembering the pie when she was talking to him and thinking about that redhead and it made her too abrupt. That's okay though. It helped her be firm and say what she meant with some conviction.

Stepping into her house she is welcomed by the aroma of cinnamon and freshly baked apple pie. Rushing to the kitchen without taking off her coat, she retrieves the pie from the oven, much relieved to see that it is nicely browned and not at all burnt. She considers cutting a piece and cooling it in the freezer so she won't have to wait, but decides to eat the last piece of lemon bundt cake instead. And after all, the cake is kind of an historical item, since she made it before she even met Leif. A good keeper, that cake. It's the oil that does it. She finds it still delicious with her coffee.

"Minnie Mouse," she says fondly, petting her fat red cat and setting the plate of crumbs on the floor, considering how she would look on the picture phone showing off her perfect apple pie, or maybe holding up Minnie Mouse wearing her new pink sparkle bow.

———

LILLY, MORGAN, AND CARMEN take turns with the binoculars at Hawk Ridge. Morgan is exhilarated after spotting a peregrine falcon, and it takes the edge off his exasperation with Carmen. After one night in Duluth she has already joined a group counting migratory birds, as well as the Save Spirit Mountaineers. Why does she always make herself so at home? Resentfully, yet with a resigned respect, he hands the binoculars to Carmen. She scans the hills below like a hawk, pausing to jot down sightings in her field book.

1 Coopers hawk

1 Peregrine falcon

1 Northern hawk owl

"I just love birds," Lilly says, lightly flapping her scarf with the pumping motion of a delicate bird. "And all these wonderful colorful trees in the snow! What a beautiful city."

Morgan says it's the maples. The rainfall and soil here are perfect for maples. He distinctly remembers that Sarah loves maple leaves. He makes a note to find some perfect red leaves for her, yes, after lunch he'll ditch Carmen, somehow. He'll get away. He snaps his fingers, then claps. How childish he's being, how out of control. With Lilly here his world is out of kilter. He knows she's trying to help him get back. But Carmen's hair. It's like the maple leaves, red and bronze in the sun. He can't help but stare.

"Do you agree?" Carmen asks. "Morgan?"

"What? Oh, I'm sorry. I was thinking."

Carmen laughs.

"Where do you live, Carmen?" Lilly asks, stepping up close to confront Carmen. "You seem so happy and at home right here. Are you like that everywhere? Or is it just Morgan?"

*part 2*

CHRISTMAS

# *one*

STEPHEN LETS THE PHONE RING several times before giving up. Irritated, he slams the phone into its cradle. He hates these airport phones. His cell is probably on the kitchen table where he set it out so he wouldn't forget. Jeannie would have hers. She certainly would, if she weren't dead. She'd be right here beside him at the Duluth airport making calls and he wouldn't be trying to call Gigi or Sarah. He should have planned better, talked to his cousin last night. Now Jim's working and he has to rent a car. He should start driving from the cities. Still, flying is faster.

And he should have sent flowers to Sarah when she was in the hospital. It was Gigi who called to tell him about the accident. He was excited, hearing Gigi on the phone; thought she wanted to see him, talk to him, but then it was about Sarah's accident. He could have sent a plant to the house or maybe a card. Had he sent a card? No, he hadn't bothered with that either. He'll get some flowers.

For a moment he senses Jeannie behind him and turns quickly. No one, of course. Just a passenger with too many bags, brushing too close. No one at all. So many times they stood here together at the airport, casual and happy, everything going according to plan. No concern about calls, luggage, cars. There was just the excitement of being on vacation, and the exhilarating first view of Lake Superior. The ease of happiness was taken for granted.

"Sir?" The car rental clerk brings Stephen out of his reverie. He slides his Yale Visa card back into his wallet. At least that gives him a twinge of pleasure as well as an occasional free flight. Too many cards. He must deal with this card clutter and get rid of some, and stop carrying Jeannie's library card, for one thing. He'd like a calling card to the dead. Or e-mail. No, a special cell phone with a button for calling the spirit world. They've given him a white car. Now he'll disappear in a snow storm. He should have insisted on red.

He sets the pasta maker for his aunt far back in the trunk, wedging it safely in place with his suitcase. He'll wrap it tonight. Better stop for paper. Jim never has anything like that since he never bothers wrapping presents. Stephen slams the trunk door harder than necessary, harder than he meant. Lately he has taken to slamming things: doors, cupboards, even refrigerator doors. He doesn't mean to do it and at the same time he does and he recognizes it as one of his new deviant quirks.

The snow is higher than usual for so early in the season. The snow banks are door-handle high. There is something quiet about snow, and Stephen likes that – seeing the forests deep in snow and the meadows and hills all smooth and white. There is little traffic on the airport road and he begins to relax. The sky is a pale winter blue over the peaceful expanse of the half-frozen lake, and thoughts of shipping and the spring thaw are buried winter deep.

The Kenwood SuperOne parking lot is half full when he pulls in, and he sees a few cars with Christmas trees sticking out of their trunks or strapped on top. A pickup truck in the next row is piled high with trees, and beside it is another truck filled with tree-length birch logs. He nearly loses his balance on a carrot in the snow when he steps out of the rental car. It still has its green stem.

Inside the store, he is still laughing quietly to himself over the carrot as he peruses the aisles for Christmas paper, oblivious to the shoppers who give him a look and steer out of his way, except for one woman who smiles back at him. Probably a person chuckling to himself in the jumper cable and dog food aisle is someone to be avoided in the cold hard month of December. Probably he is someone to be avoided. Why is he laughing about a carrot he could have slipped on? He could have ended up with a broken leg. Spent Christmas in the hospital. He finds the wrapping paper around the corner, and chooses a fat roll of blue paper with snowmen, the kind of paper Jeannie would have called childish.

Next, from the frozen food section, he grabs two large-sized packages of frozen shrimp, and then a jar of sauce, and finally a box of chocolate-covered doughnuts for Jim. Stephen finds himself in the produce department, pondering the carrots and other brightly-colored vegetables. He doesn't remember steering his cart here, but here he is, as if possessed by some carrot spirit. Carrots mean nothing to him. He doesn't even like them. Well, he eats them, if someone prepares them, but they have an unpleasant bitter taste and he finds it odd that a root vegetable that grows in the ground has such a bright color, like a flower or some cheerful plant that grows in the sun. Abruptly, he snatches a large bag of carrots and heads for the checkout counter. At the end of the aisle he spots Poinsettias on sale. They look healthy. He picks a big red one for Sarah with her poor broken back.

"Oh, you'll have to wrap that in a big bag. It'll freeze if you don't," the woman in line behind him offers, the same woman who smiled at him earlier.

"She's right," the clerk adds.

"Blow in the bag. Get your hot air into the bag, then close her up tight. A rubber band or a twister tie – either's okay. Poinsettias are touchy."

Before leaving the store, Stephen sets his grocery bag on the ledge by the Bugeteers and starts to blow into the plastic bag until it balloons open. He quickly places it over the poinsettia, but he's not quick enough and it deflates. The lady from the line comes up behind him. "Like this," she says, tucking the bag around the plant and forming a crinkly funnel. Stephen holds the stem of the bag and blows until it balloons out and this time he holds it securely while he tightens the end with a metal twister.

"Good job," she congratulates him on his success. "Hope it don't turn black on you," she adds, then laughs a loud, good-natured laugh as she leaves through the automatic door. With the groceries in his right hand and the poinsettia in his left, he hurries to his white rental car in the snow. The carrot he stepped on earlier is nowhere in sight.

There's a light on in the front of Lilly's house. No time to have called ahead, he'll just take a chance. This time he remembers the doorbell doesn't work so he knocks loudly, almost frantically. Tom Troll lets him in. He starts right in when he sees Sarah nestled in a blanket on the chaise longue until Tom reminds him of Lilly's "no shoes in the house" rule and he unlaces his boots and sets them on the cedar shoe rack in the entry way.

"She's asleep," Tom tells him, but after seeing his disappointment, says he can sit with him for a short time to see if she will wake up. They sit in chairs near Sarah, and Stephen opens the plastic bag protecting the plant. He is relieved to see that it's still red and fresh, and he is proud of himself for having chosen such a beautiful flowering plant for Sarah.

They talk in whispers, and hearing that Tom is actually Tom Troll of the Taxidermy shop over on Sixth Avenue, Stephen is incredulous. He can't get over how this is the legendary Tom Troll, the taxidermist. But this must be the son. Yes, it must have been Tom's father he used to pay each Saturday night, going to the side workshop door of the taxidermy shop and handing over his five dollar bill. He had backed into a car one slippery winter evening when he was still a new driver, back in high school. The owner of the car he hit was Tom Troll, Sr., the famed taxidermist who stuffed the black bear of Hotel Duluth's Black Bear Lounge, after it wandered into the hotel one cold fall day of misfortune for the bear.

Stephen handed over his five every Saturday night all winter long, and was never invited past the workshop door. He remembers standing in the cold with the bill folded inside his glove, and the smell of a wood-burning fire from within. Mr. Troll would smile and thank him kindly, then close the door with a stern look, which he took as a reprimand for his careless driving, though it was icy that night and probably even an experienced driver would have slid as he had. But from the doorway he saw various details of the taxidermy trade. He remembers the tails of dead creatures hanging down from a beam, and the dark silhouette of a moose's big nose and antlers. Now, looking down at his gray-stockinged feet, he recalls a glimpse of a goose, and its wings flopped over the edge of a wooden counter top, and the light with that old-fashioned golden glow, likely from a kerosene lamp. Yet it had seemed to him that it was a scene from a children's book come to life, and he was intrigued and never afraid and each Saturday night he hoped Mr. Troll would invite him inside. He had decided to ask to see the workshop when he came with his last payment, but the shop was closed that night and he ended up sending the last five by mail.

Over the course of the winter he gathered a collection of details from his brief visits, and his mind had filled in many of the blanks, yet he still had a desire to see the inside of the taxidermy shop. Was this a longing for some childhood picture book dream, or was it a need to see more clearly the stark cold details of death? Wasn't it similar to having glimpses into the back room of Johnson's Mortuary down on Fourth Street? Wasn't it just a natural and irresistible curiosity? Of course he had only seen the open door of the mortuary from afar, and just a time or two on his way home from his friend Russell Wobble's house, such a long time ago.

Tom seems to have no blood on his hands. He sits comfortably in the quiet, much like a Tibetan priest Stephen sat beside at an airport once, and this calm makes Stephen want to sit there all night watching over the sleeping Sarah. He hasn't felt so at home, so comfortable, for a long time. Sarah's shoulder seems of the utmost interest to him, covered in a soft lavender material like fur which he'd like to touch, just softly like he might pet a cat, to make her better, to calm her dreams, to calm his own. Her hair is soft and silky and the way the light shines it looks blue, but of course not really blue. It must be the effect of the Tiffany lamp, he's sure. Stephen feels himself leaning, almost falling off his chair toward Sarah. In almost a whisper, Tom asks him what he does, in Minneapolis.

"I teach," he says, feeling no need to elaborate, as is his usual custom. Tom looks at him, through him, beyond him, but it doesn't make Stephen uncomfortable. Is this the nature of taxidermists? Are they our northern priests, soothsayers and guides? Unexpectedly, he finds himself reddening, as if Sam knows everything about him, even his Madonna rituals.

"I'd better go," he tells Tom. "Tell Sarah I stopped by to wish her a Merry Christmas." On the boot rack his boots look peculiar, though surely no different than when he took them off. He doesn't know why he hesitates. Is he expecting a poisonous spider in the toe of his boat? One of Morgan's souvenirs from the jungle?

"Are you all right," Tom asks. "Is there anything I can do?"

"I'm fine, thanks," Stephen says, stepping into his boots.

In the car again he feels out of control. "Tell her I love her, tell her I'm half mad," he mumbles in the cold air of the empty car. He finds himself laughing again, like in the grocery store over the carrot. "Spider Man. I'm Spider Man," he sings loudly and dramatically, trying for the inflection of the man who eats flies in Dracula. Who is that actor? He can just see the guy. Dwight Frye, yes, even his name is creepy. He plays Renfield, the spider man, yes. It cheers him to think of that funny little man, such a marvelous actor, snapping out at flies with his thin black lips and those wild, insane eyes. Stephen is thoroughly jovial by the time he pulls into the alley behind his cousin's house.

He'll thaw the shrimp and they can eat when Jim gets home. And wrap the presents – the fishing knife he bought for Jim and the pasta maker for his Aunt Ellie, then he'll be ready for an early start in the morning. He would like to get to Ely by mid-afternoon. First, he had better call Hawk, before Jim gets back – then he'll do the wrapping.

"No. Hawk's not here."

"I need to talk to him. He's expecting my call. When will he be back?"

"Hard to tell. He's in the woods. Today, tomorrow. Maybe New Year's. When he goes to the woods you never know. He could stay one day, sometimes all winter."

"But I have to talk to him. My name is Stephen. Stephen Spine. Maybe he left a message for me"

"No message."

Okay. I'll call tomorrow. And your name?"

Barrow."

"Well thanks, Barrow. Tell Hawk I'll call tomorrow. I mean if he comes back. Just tell him I'll call tomorrow." Stephen hesitates before telling Barrow to mention that he has the money.

Barrow hangs up abruptly, leaving Stephen listening to the drone of the dial tone, unsure if he heard what he said about the money.

He should have been there. He promised. Said he would have it. He held up his end of the bargain. The money, every bill, already in an envelope, counted and recounted. Stephen puts on his coat and leaves the house, slamming the door behind him. "Shit," he plops down onto the cold car seat.

---

LAKE AVENUE SEEMS STEEPER than usual, steeper in the dark. The bridge glows silver under the night lights. There is no wait for a ship, of course, at this time of year. He doesn't need to go to the end; doesn't need to walk along the beach in the dark. Not yet, not without his new sculpture. What if he doesn't get it? Hawk. How can he count on someone like that? Stephen turns short at the bridge and drives past Grandma's Restaurant and parks beside the pier. He grabs his Russian fur hat from the back seat. Thank God there's no wind. It's cold enough as it is. The pier is deserted and he walks rapidly toward its end. Halfway, he pauses to look at the lights of the city above him, twinkling and colorful over the hills of Duluth. The red lights of the tall TV and radio towers look festive and Christmassy. Every house seems to be sparkling with lights, glowing with happy people inside ready to celebrate the season, all except him. Everyone but Stephen. The downtown lights glitter in the lake in long watery ripples, reflecting the city's beauty, and the lights in Lake Superior seems as deep as the knives piercing his cold and lonely heart.

"Upside down Christmas trees," says a small crackly voice beside him. "Those lights in the water. You jumpin?"

The little man beside him wears a black coat much too large for his slight frame.

"In the lake, you mean?" Stephen responds.

"Sure. Gitche Gumee. Lake Superior. I come here every year. My brother's in the lake. I just come down here and talk to him. He went down with the *Edmund Fitzgerald.* I've never missed a year since she went down on November 20, 1975. Long time now. All 29 men lost. Maybe *I'll* jump. One of these years, that's probably what I'll do. By the time I'm ready, I'll be too decrepit to get over the edge. Too old to get myself down here even." The old man laughs a sad quiet laugh.

"But you won't jump this year," Stephen says, horrified at the possibility, even if he is unsure of what he's doing here himself.

"No, not this year. I see people though. Lonely folks thinking about it. Folks like yourself. Mostly they don't. Something about the cold gray water makes them stop. It comforts them – talks to them is what I think. The lake, and those lights so pretty like that. Like Christmas trees, all those reflections of Duluth in the water. Sometimes it's completely froze up by now. Blue ice. Green ice. Or white ice, clear up to the shore. That's when you see the ghosts – specially when the ice is green, a real spooky green. Brrrr. Not this year though."

"Over there, my great uncle's best friend drowned. He used to swim here between the piers, he and his brother. They'd dive in from right over there, on the harbor side. Hit a log is what happened. Big log drifting under the water, real waterlogged and just deep enough so's he couldn't see it. Dived here all the time up till then."

"And at the very end of the pier, the Halvorsen boys went down. They were out looking at a storm, like kids do, and the big waves just took 'em. Coast Guard tried to help, but all three drowned. All three brothers."

Stephen remembered the story. So sad.

"That was at the end of this very pier. My brother was never found." The little man leans his head on the cement pier and begins to cry.

The sound of the waves against the pier suddenly looms large, even though the waves are gentle. To end the crying Stephen asks the man if knew the Halvorsen boys.

"Oh no," he says through his sniffling. "Nope. Didn't know those boys. Maybe I know them a little, from the lake, from coming here all these years. I've come to believe the water is our home, from where we all come and where we all go. When we die, we turn into rain. The human body is over half water. I read that. I lose two percent every year crying on this pier. The brain is mostly water. That's another fact. Hardly anyone knows that one. They brought up the bell in 1995, from the *Fitzgerald*. I go see it every summer, over in Michigan, in the White Fish Point Museum. She went down off White Fish Point."

"I don't know why I'm here," Stephen says, pulling his hat down over his ears. "I just came here. I guess I'm one of those lonely people you see now and then," and Stephen feels better for having said so, even if he is sorry for the drowned and those who mourn.

The little man smiles and draws his head into his coat like a turtle. He begins humming in a high reedy monotone, which makes Stephen think of a boat whistle, a far off boat whistle from under a frozen lake; maybe the ghost whistle of the *S.S. Edmund Fitzgerald* itself. Stephen takes it as a signal for his departure and he bids the man of the pier a good night.

Heading toward his car, he pauses at the sound of music coming from a lighted building on the far side of the parking lot. He is quite sure the music is coming from the coffee shop in the lower level of the DeWitte Seitz shopping center, where he spent an evening last summer with Gigi. They heard Leo Kottke, the guitar player. Unfortunately, he also sang, and Stephen had thought he could sing as well himself. But he hadn't minded. It made Kottke seem more human, and he liked that. Amazing Grace, that's the name of the coffee shop. He had ordered a large bowl of hearty barley soup, and a giant cookie, and the healthy soup and the decadent sweet seemed to balance one another, much like Leo Kottke's singing and guitar playing. They've started a new song: Oh Come All Ye Faithful, and Stephen joins in on the refrain in the cold night of the parking lot. He continues humming as he settles himself inside his freezing cold car, wishing it had a heated seat feature. He's cold now but happy, or at least moderately happy. As he pulls away he sees the small dark shape of the little man walking toward the end of the pier.

———  ———  ———

STEPHEN CANNOT RECALL when he last had such energy. Here he is, halfway to the Iron Range and the sun is just rising. He might as well be driving into a calendar scene, the way the sky and snow on the trees has turned completely pink. What a beautiful morning. And to think that last night he was in such despair. Two deer at the side of the road leap into the forest, their white tails pink from the morning sun. He decides to slow down. He's been driving too fast.

He's glad he called Sarah before he went to bed. She loved the poinsettias, and was glad he had stopped by. She sounded happier and healthier even, which surprised him. Somehow he thought that after the accident she would sound feeble and weak of voice and spirit. Sarah had read him her aunt's e-mail from India and she had ended up laughing so hard he could hardly follow what she said. Lilly had written about a monkey in the courtyard, all wound up and playing and prancing around in Lilly's gold sari which she had hung out to dry. Then she had to bribe the monkey by rolling oranges out into the yard so she could catch an edge of the gold silk and unwind it from the mischief maker.

As he drives North, Stephen thinks of the monkey leaping about in a gold sari and Lilly with the oranges, and the world feels small and joyful and he feels almost normal. If only he could do nothing but drive, just keep driving through this northern forest, on and on deeper into the forest, deeper into the cold and the endless snow.

———  ———  ———

MEANWHILE, HAWK IS SEATED at a work bench in his cabin, hunched over a wooden form. There are cans of paint and an assortment of brushes beside him on the table, and he is intent as he sands the form taking shape. Nearby are cans of crackling glaze, antiquing powder, gold leaf, and his tin of chewing tobacco. The log wall behind him is covered with masks, totems, crucifixes, old metal traps, skis, snowshoes and a big poster in Spanish advertising a bullfight from 1989. A well-made ladder leads to a sleeping loft. Two stoves sit side by side, with fires flickering from each, one a small pot-bellied stove and the other an enameled turquoise-blue stove. Together they provide adequate heat for the cabin as Hawk is in a short-sleeved T-shirt sporting a grinning Dracula. A coffee pot and an old Hills Brothers coffee can of bacon grease sit at the back of the blue stove.

Hawk stretches and rolls his shoulders before taking the pan of baking powder biscuits out of the oven. He whacks the biscuits out onto the table and walks around the room eating. While he circles the table, he focuses on the Madonna, whose beatific smile makes him pause. He's done a good job. He fiddles with the radio dial until he finds the Canadian station with the guy who reads short stories. He pulls up his socks, pours a cup of coffee, and settles into his cracked leather chair. Life is good, here in the forest.

———

THE CHIPMUNKS' CHRISTMAS SONG is playing on the radio as Stephen pulls into Ely just before dark. "*I still want a hula hoop.*" Unfortunately he left his CDs in his cousin's kitchen when he left Duluth, not quite awake at 6:00 a.m. "*Please Christmas don't be late.*" Still, it was a good day, a good drive, even though he spent far too long visiting his old pal, Andrew, in Virginia. Their lunch was satisfactory, and all the reminiscing was enjoyable. Andrew still has the same job he took right out of college, teaching English at Virginia's high school. He's such a happy guy. He loves teaching, loves fishing, his family, his garden, his furniture. Even his dog seems happy and well adjusted. Stephen sighs loudly. *"I still want a hula hoop."*

Central Avenue in Ely is as quiet as snow. There's not a soul in sight, neither on the street nor in the stores, which are all closed, although a smattering of Christmas lights are still on, giving a festive look to the deserted downtown. At each corner, garlands of pine with tasteful tiny white lights circle the light posts. Stephen pauses in front of a store window where a mannequin is dressed in a bathing suit, snowshoes and Santa hat, holding a canoe paddle with a sign advertising a Christmas canoe sale. Stephen winces, seeing the scantily clad form, even if it is only a dummy. He knows from the radio that it is currently seven degrees below zero. Stephen drives up and down the streets, past the Northern Grounds, The Moose, past Cranberry's, and Pizza Hut. "The Hobbit" is playing at the State Theater.

The houses in Ely are lit up with decorations and Christmas trees, which are all the more dramatic for the snow, as darkness settles over the town. Stephen stops and sits quietly in front of his aunt's house. The lights of her Christmas tree look much like the lights of the trees in the other houses, but to Stephen her lights are warmer and brighter. Her hearing has been failing these last years, and she hasn't heard him drive up. He sees her bustle past the window back in the kitchen. She's wearing a dark dress and a white apron which outlines and amplifies her ample figure. And yes, she has a drink in hand. Same old Aunt Ellie. Happy hour in Ely; gin and tonic time.

She spots him from the picture window when he starts down the narrow sidewalk to the house, and hurries to open the door, her plump joyous arms held out in greeting. "Stevie, my dear Stevie," she hugs him soundly and little Bluebell, her yippy Chihuahua, same as always, barks and jumps in a dither, though not so high as before, now a bit older and plumper, yet still crazy with aggressive barking and a fiercely wagging tail. He accepts it all, Silent Night, Holy Happy Night; he's loved, more or less, he's home. Before he gets his coat off, Ellie has poured him a seriously large gin and tonic, "with a twist," she says, chuckling, already enjoying the opportunity to fuss over her favorite nephew.

They settle down in the living room with their TV trays in front of the big velvet couch and feast on mallard, done just the way Stephen loves it. There is also wild rice with butter, cranberry sauce, mashed potatoes and mushroom gravy, and stewed tomatoes. She insists on adding olives to their gin and tonics, and after two, Stephen agrees that is the way they should be served, at least on Christmas. Bluebell has her own dish of duck, with a pit less black olive on the side, which, strangely enough, she actually eats.

The evening passes quickly, or so it seems. To hell with the headache he's certain to have in the morning. Ellie's arms are thrown back and draped along the top of the couch and Bluebell is asleep beside her wobbly thigh under a crumpled red wrapping tissue, a slimy chew stick tucked under her chin. His aunt's crooked sleeping lips, relaxed into a half grin, make her look like Stan from the Laurel and Hardy movies – one of those episodes whey they played themselves as well as their look-alike twin wives. Of course, his aunt is a big woman, but still, it's Stan she resembles. Her knitting rests on her lap, though Stephen doesn't know how she could have been knitting after all those G & Ts. As long as he's known her she has always been working on a baby blanket. "For baby Joey," she would say, the baby she never had, and he wonders just how many baby quilts she has knit for charities over the years. He pictures hundreds of babies around the world, hundreds of baby Joeys comforted in her pink and blue and yellow blankets, a regular UNICEF panorama of happy warm babies. Oh, he does love his Aunt Ellie.

She won't mind if he cuts a piece, he's sure, as he takes a beautiful lattice-topped blueberry pie out of the fridge. Sure enough, two kinds of ice cream in the freezer: vanilla, and she's bought his favorite, Ben & Jerry's Cherry Garcia. Vanilla for the pie though, for his extra large quarter-of-a pie sized slice of homemade wild blueberry pie. The purple juice oozes onto the plate. What a glutton you are, Stephen, he tells himself in his gin and tonic haziness, scolding himself like a child. Heavenly, this first bite, even better than he remembered. He could die happily with the taste of Aunt Ellie's blueberry pie in his mouth. What a perfect way to end Christmas Eve.

"Well Bluebell, you want some too? Here you go." Stephen drops a gooey blueberry and Bluebell catches it before it hits the floor. She eats the blueberry like she has a hot potato in her mouth, shuffling it around, before swallowing in one gulp.

"Oh Geez," Stephen groans, seeing Bluebell run to the back door, looking up at him expectantly. He slips on his coat and steps into his boots. As soon as he opens the door Bluebell darts outside and disappears. Vanished. Where'd she go? There's nothing but snow. This is the last house on the block, bordering the woods. Even with the porch light on, he can't see the dog. There are no tracks, except a couple on the porch. He hears a muffled bark in the snow. She's sunk down out of sight, but where? He reaches down in the vicinity of the bark with his bare hand. Darn cold. Snow, more snow, and a stem of some kind, some prickly plant, and more snow. It's like she had been caught in an avalanche.

What if he can't find her? What if she dies, and on Christmas Eve? Just don't panic – keep looking. She has to be somewhere. He widens his search listening for another bark. Hearing a feeble yip, he reaches deep into the snow. Fur, a leg, he's got her! Stephen picks up the Chihuahua and brushes off the snow, holds her to his chest and brings her back inside, shutting the door quietly so as not to wake his aunt from her slumber on the couch. Thank heavens, she doesn't wake. Stephen sets Bluebell on top of his coat next to the register in the kitchen and pulls up a chair near the shivering dog. After a few minutes she has climbed into a sleeve and has stopped shivering, her long nose poking out from the cave of the coat sleeve. She sighs, curls up, and falls asleep.

---

THE NEXT MORNING, Stephen is up early. He plans to wash all the dishes in the quiet kitchen before his aunt gets up. He'll clean and wash away his guilt from almost killing the dog, now apparently upstairs sleeping with his aunt. And amazingly, he has no headache this morning, knock on wood. He gathers up glasses, bowls of nuts and empty plates from the living room. He loves the look and feel of a party when it's over. Jeannie used to go straight to bed after their parties, not that they had all that many, but there was always New Year's Eve, and at least one summer party, sometimes two. He liked the candle light shining on all the empty glasses and he would let them burn down while he picked up around the house. It was his magic hour, and he walked around sleepy and grinning to himself, remembering the guests, their laughter, little anecdotes of the evening, and how pretty Jeannie had looked. It was all part of his own little play in the quiet empty house, when he could talk to himself, or talk to the furniture, for that matter. His old purple easy chair seemed like a true friend, sitting there in the night all by itself with open arms. And the dark woodwork of the house never looked better than in the candlelight – so atmospheric, so Edgar Allen Poe, especially the fireplace.

He liked to gather up the glasses on a silver tray, and pour bits of leftover wine, Manhattans, beer, whatever, into one of the glasses and then hold up the concoction in a private quiet toast which he never actually drank. "To Dr. Doolittle," he would say, though he was thinking of "Doc" in Steinbeck's "Cannery Row." And that became a habit, that sly toast which he poured down the drain. "To Dr. Doolittle," he says as he pours the leftover gin and tonic, mostly melted ice now mixed with cold coffee, down his Aunt Ellie's drain.

Those odd little things he likes to do, he wonders, are they the things that express his spirit, his real self? Rubbing his hands together, he rubs away at whatever he needs to rub away, or rub into being. Hawk must be back by now, but he can't call yet. He'd better wait at least until 7:00 o'clock. He doesn't want to sound desperate. With a tingling at the nape of his neck, Stephen feels his other self, his new seedy self, slither into his skin. He dashes quietly up the stairs to count his money.

# two

SARA AND MORGAN ARE having breakfast. Sam is in the next room sitting in meditation under the lavender turban he's recently taken to wearing in the house. Sarah is taking notes from Craigslist of free items while she eats her cereal. Morgan is reading aloud about seagulls, and in particular, a non-native gull which is taking over in the harbor. Sarah looks up but he can tell she's not really listening. He doesn't mind. He puts down the magazine and finishes his tea, a strong Lapsong Souchong that Lilly sent in a recent package, which included the pale blue sari Sarah is wearing this morning. She looks really good in those saris, and he finds himself staring. He likes that Sarah doesn't notice. Carmen would notice. But then she wouldn't wear a sari. She always wears Khaki, and for formal occasions, those odd Khaki suits without buttons. She would look strange in a sari anyway.

Carmen just won't go away, but he's aware that she's receding, and seems further away each time he sees her until she's barely there, even though she is. Carmen doesn't know she's fading away. He likes it here with Sarah, just sitting and sipping his tea. He likes that pale blue, all loose and silky. Here he doesn't even have to talk. The tea has an earthy, smoky flavor which he is starting to associate with Duluth, and these cozy breakfasts. He prefers a loose tea like this as being more natural and less refined. Carmen is more of a tea bag person, which seems more pretentious. Funny how he never noticed that before. Funny how he's noticing things like that. Some mornings he feels like he's seeing Sarah for the first time.

"Free goat hay" she says, then laughs and adds it to her list. So far for the week she has added:

Free peanut oil, 5.5 gal.

Free hot tub – leaks

Old Tires – Highway 50

2 free frogs and tank

Free roosters

Free used bowling pins

"Another free piano," she says. That's sad. A sign of the times." They've talked about this before, the unwanted pianos and organs, both agreeing everyone should be able to play an instrument and make music. Morgan decided to bring back a flute for Sarah when he checks on the remodeling of the Park Point house. This might be just the right time for a flute. She needs something.

He's anxious to see how the house is coming along, but he won't leave until Sam finishes with the yoga lesson and Sam is out of the house. He either plays the piano or reads during the lessons, and sometimes he joins in. Just this week Sarah has begun to look less stiff and more relaxed in her upper body. She's been without the back brace for nearly a month now. Before, she would go a little longer each day without the brace, until she could go all day without it. At first she said she felt unsafe without the brace, like a beetle without its shell – quite naked and vulnerable. Morgan tries to understand, and not rush her along. He's familiar with many species of beetles.

They begin with breathing exercises, and chanting. Morgan can't stand Sam's chanting. His voice is just plain ugly – even worse than his speaking voice. Lilly has a lovely voice and he has always enjoyed her chants. Once they were driving back from Thunder Bay and as the evening sky turned a brilliant red, Lilly burst into song in the form of a chant. He's always liked her for her appreciation of nature, and her unself-conscious ways. Sarah is becoming much more like her, or maybe she always was like Lilly and he never noticed, never appreciated.

Morgan works on the house plans during the remainder of the yoga session. He wants the upper deck of the house shielded from the screen house so you have a direct view to the lake. He is considering a small tower and is waiting for approval of his plan. The top room of the tower could revolve, making an excellent observatory which he would make available to UMD and the University of Wisconsin on occasions of particular stellar interest.

---

SARAH HAS THE HOUSE to herself. She is looking forward to their new house on Park Point, which is not really new, but is a nearly complete redoing of the old home. Morgan loves overseeing all aspects of construction, and occasionally joins in to help. Sarah has decided to stay away until it is finished. Seeing all of the interior structures makes her uncomfortable. Still, she likes to think of how pleasant it will be to have breakfast while looking out at the great expanse of Lake Superior and to be able to hear the waves schussing over the sand in summer. Just the idea of water is comforting to her, and especially as she considers her back. She often feels that she is basically a spine – a walking spine, and has been working hard toward its renewal. In the shower she lets the hot water run down her back longer than usual, mesmerized by its soothing warmth as she ponders her own spine, spines in general, and the spines of creatures of the sea. Is there some genetic memory that makes her look with such longing when she stands on the shores of a lake? It's not the other side she wants to reach; it's the water itself she is drawn to.

The African violet Tom Troll brought at Christmas has started to bloom. She's been watering it with just a teaspoon of water every third day, as Lilly suggested. She sets it on the desk next to Stephen's Poinsettia and gets a second cup of tea, then settles down to check her e-mail. There is a new message from Lilly about how the monkeys of India are like Duluth's backyard squirrels, both *"very clever and mischievous, aren't they."* She can almost hear Lilly's voice as she reads the words. Sam Light's Thought for the Day is "Try something new today." Okay, she'll think about that. Better than yesterday, which was about the summer flowers in one's heart. Hard to consider with the outdoor temperature below zero already. One thing is certain and that is that Sam is no Wordsworth.

Morgan has been polite to Sam, as he is to everyone, but she can tell he doesn't like him. But Sam is a good teacher for her. He is patient and seems to know exactly how far she can go on a particular day. She feels safe working with him. This week she has been working on the small muscles of her lower spine which lost considerable strength while she wore the brace. But some of the leg lifts seem too easy, like baby exercises. She needs to restrain herself in order to raise her legs only an inch or two off the floor and no higher. Sam explained how the large muscles kick in if you go too high, and she needs to work on the small muscles. He chooses just what she needs, just when she needs it.

Shortly after her hospital stay, when she was newly in the brace and basically immobilized, he had her do a Tai Chi exercise that filled her with energy and hope. While lying in bed she would lift an invisible ball of energy up toward the sky, then slowly lower it down. She did this several times, and was happy to be able to accomplish such simple movements. Each time she moved the invisible ball, something inexplicable and lovely filled her with a cosmic energy and connected her to a world beyond her own little bedroom. She's come a long way.

Standing at the window, she watches the downtown bus go by. She's been watching it go by for the last two weeks and knows it passes the corner once every hour. It's cold out but sunny, so why not? She could be ready in time for the next bus, ready for something new.

---

"SARAH," MORGAN CALLS as he steps out of his boots and hurries to the study where she likes to nap in the afternoons. Odd, she's usually still asleep. "Sarah," he calls again, walking from room to room. She wouldn't have gone outside, not in the snow. How very odd. Still, he puts on his boots and steps outside, looking for footsteps in the snow in the front, back and side yards. He checks the shed and the old garage. There are no steps leading to the creek. There's probably a note. Yes, of course. He should have checked for that first. Back inside, he looks around the kitchen, on the countertop, the refrigerator, the table by her napping bed. Nothing. The coffee maker is still on. And for who? They never make coffee for themselves, both confirmed tea drinkers for some years now.

Damn, that Sam. If she's with him. But that's probably where she is – out for a drive, something like that. Irritated but not unduly concerned, Morgan turns off the coffee maker and pours the leftovers down the drain. He pours himself a brandy and sits at the kitchen table to look over the photos of the house he's anxious to show Sarah. He picked up the pictures at the drug store on his way home and now slides them out of the Walgreen's envelope. The first photo is of the new house on the snowy beach from the lake and the sky is as blue as a blue bird, a good picture. He flips through the photos, pausing at the new bathroom. The upstairs bath is unfinished. He makes a note to be sure the faucet is on the lake end when they set in the tub so they will have a direct view of the lake while soaking in the bath.

And won't Sarah be surprised to see how her fish tank idea is coming along! Taking a shower beside a floor to ceiling fish tank will be like taking a shower with fish, as in her dream. Very creative, yes a clever idea, and Morgan smiles at the photo of the unfinished shower stall beside the aquarium. In her dream the fish were gold. He'll find some beautiful gold fish for Sarah, and introduce her to a few new species as well. Or they can choose the fish together, from the new tropical fish store on Lake Avenue.

Morgan checks the new answering machine. Lulu and Leif called from an ice house on Fish Lake. Lulu doesn't understand that you need a phone compatible to both the caller and the receiver. Still, he has to smile, she's so enthusiastic, describing how she's holding the phone out so Sarah can see the carpeting in Leif's fish house, a nice green, like grass, she says.

The second message is short and curt, a man's voice, unfamiliar. Abrupt, with a peculiar accent.

"It's Hawk. I got it. Meet me Saturday. Twelve o'clock at the fish house. Bring the money."

Morgan can hear the phone slam at the end of the message. Who the hell is that? A joke, wrong number? What kind of a name is Hawk? Now Sam might get a call like that. Never trusted the guy. Never. Morgan jots down Hawk's number and checks the phone book to see where the call is from. It's an Ely extension which covers most of the Boundary Waters Canoe Area, including Lake Kabetogama and the Gunflint Trail and on over toward Grand Marais. Could be any of many towns. Or a cell phone. What fish house?

He has a cold feeling in his gut and is suddenly aware of a metallic taste in his own saliva. Turn up the heat, that's what he'll do, warm it up. And play something. She'll be back soon – it'll be dark in an hour. Of course she'll be back. Wrong number, certainly. They don't know any Hawk. He slips on his favorite Norwegian sweater, the black and white with the ragged cuffs, and opens the piano top. He plays Mozart's Concerto No. 23 to the empty house. As he finishes, the phone rings. He almost slips on the kitchen floor rushing to answer. It's Carmen.

"Carmen, go away." He hangs up, surprising himself. He really means it. Yesterday, in that green sweater she looked like a Praying Mantis. And he's tired of all her teeth – way too many perfect white teeth. Amazingly, she doesn't call back, and Morgan is aware of the silence in the room. He could do something, maybe drive around town, stop at places Sarah might go, but then she could return while he's out. Or he could make some calls. But then Sarah might call. He makes a list of people to call, just in case – Sam Light, Lulu, Sarah's old friend Gigi, and Julia, the hot dish singer. But he doesn't know their last names, not even Lulu's. That leaves Sam, and yes, Tom Troll, the taxidermist. Now he's a good man, even if his business is a ghoulish one. So why do only the men have last names?

Stephen Spine. The professor, certainly. He knows Sarah, knows her well. He'll call Stephen's cousin, just in case. Sarah said he always stays with the cousin – they have the same last name, yes, he's in the book. Morgan folds up his list and slips it into his pocket. He wouldn't want her to think he has been overly worried, if she returns soon.

Morgan looks out the window toward the street, hoping to see her drive in with someone, even if it is Sam. It's too quiet in the house. He heads to the cellar for potatoes. He'll make a big pot of soup. She loves potato soup.

Lilly's cellar is dark and cool, with wooden shelves of jams and jellies, pickles, and canned fruit in glass jars lined up in rows. It's like a shrine to fruit, with peaches and apricots in the center row, flanked with other shelves of raspberry, blueberry and rhubarb sauce. A tall stack of wax rectangles sits on a shelf near cans of pickles, relishes and chutneys, each with its neat handwritten label – Lilly's writing no doubt. He's intrigued by a mango-cloudberry chutney. Just what are cloudberries? His mother never did any of these things, like canning, pickling, anything domestic. They always had a cook, Martha, who came in the morning and left after dinner. She was very clean and strict. He chooses a jar of blueberry sauce, grabs the bag of potatoes and heads back upstairs.

It's dark by the time he has peeled the last potato. He chops an onion, knowing he'll have an excuse to shed a few tears, something he hasn't done in many years, not even on the flight back to Minnesota after Sarah's accident. The hot onion-induced tears sting, but they feel good too, flooding down his face. He mops them off with the kitchen towel. He calls Sam's number and gets the answering machine. Next he finds Lulu's number on a list beside the kitchen phone. She's home, but no, she hasn't seen Sarah, hasn't heard from her, but then she hasn't been home very long – it was a long drive back from Fish Lake, she tells Morgan. And Leif got one big walleye, that's all.

"You mean she's not there at all then and you don't know where she is? No note either?" Lulu says, taking in the situation as she speaks.

"That's right. I think I'd better call the police."

"Oh dear," Lulu says. "Oh dear me, Morgan. I think I'd better come over."

"Yes, thanks, Lulu. You can stay and get the phone in case I have to go out and look."

Lulu agrees to come right away, as soon as she feeds her cat. Minnie Mouse. Why does she have a cat with the name of a mouse? Strange, this Lulu. The police officer is polite, and tells Morgan to call if she's not back in the morning. There's nothing they can do until she's been missing for 24 hours. He asks if they've had a fight or if anything happened that would make her take off suddenly. As he hangs up he goes over the events of the morning but can think of nothing unusual. She was cheerful this morning. Amusing herself making those lists. She wouldn't have gone out to get one of those free things? Darndest thing. She knows she can buy whatever she likes. Anyway, she's not up to driving yet. Yes, she seemed unusually happy this morning, they both did – just very content, or so he had thought.

Maybe she went for a walk. She always liked walking at Chester Park. But no, that's way too far. But if she did, she may have fallen. Who would see her? She could have slipped, up by those thickets past the open field before you get to the woods. He'll drive slowly toward Chester Park as soon as Lulu arrives. The soup has boiled over. He sets it at the back of the stove, unable to remember what he added other than the potatoes.

Morgan paces back and forth in the living room, waiting for Lulu. She could be lying by the black stone bridge near the entrance to Chester Park; it's always slippery on a bridge. What if she hit her head on a rock and has been lying there all this time. Red blood on snow.

Morgan is in a panic by the time Lulu arrives. As soon as she hears Morgan's plan she calls Leif so he can go out and look around. Morgan had forgotten that Leif is the caretaker and lives right there in Chester Park. Leif answers on the first ring, and agrees to walk down the road past the lake and check the area around the bridge and Morgan will drive slowly toward the park checking the sides of the road.

As Morgan turns off Kenwood Avenue toward Chester Park, he slows to a crawl. There is little traffic on the road, no more than a local or two going home at this time of day. There are few homes on the lake side of the road and in his headlights the fresh white snow along the sides of the road sparkles in the cold. The sumac thickets and pines are prickly with snow crystals, as if trimmed for a winter carnival by some Nordic god. But Morgan is in no carnival mood. He feels a stiffness throughout his body as if he were made of ice. He's never driven this slow. He spots something in the snow. He gasps and pulls to a stop. Bit it is only a large rock sticking out of the snow, just a boulder, but round like a skull. Before driving on, he opens the window so he can hear, just in case. The sound of the tires on the snow-covered road seems amplified, like something you would only hear through a stethoscope, a scrunching undertone and a murmuring like the snow itself is trying to tell Morgan something he doesn't want to know. His heart pounds, seeing a jogger nonchalantly jogging toward him at the curve of the road before the black bridge. He stops the car.

"Have you seen anyone? Anyone fallen, or anything?" he calls out as the jogger nears.

"No, sorry," the jogger says, jogging in place, his moustache iced up in the cold.

"I'm looking for my wife," Morgan says. "Long hair – not too tall."

"I'll keep an eye out." The jogger nods his head and jogs on. Morgan watches the iridescent shoulder stripes move rhythmically away into the night, before driving on.

He parks at the bridge just as Leif nears its other end from Chester Park. Leif is carrying a rifle, and his small wiry frame under the street light makes him look like a soldier from some long lost winter war.

"Been under the bridge. No tracks, nothing down there," he says. "I'm no smart scientist like you, Dr. Morgan, but I don't think she'd come up here."

They lean on the railing and look at the frozen river below, at all the frozen formations of snow and ice. Morgan feels an involuntary twitch in his shoulder, thinking of Sarah shivering somewhere in her blue sari. But she wouldn't have gone out in that, surely – unless she left quickly, left against her will. When he gets back he'll tell the police about the call from that guy – Hawk. Why didn't he think of that earlier?

"Well, it seems you're right, Leif. She's not here. Thanks. I appreciate you coming to look." They shake gloved hands and Morgan walks back to his car.

"Mr. Morgan," Leif calls out. You ought to take better care of her. Lulu told me about your redhead. You ought to know better, smart man like you."

Leif shifts his rifle from hand to hand. Morgan can't keep his hand from trembling as he starts the car and drives off, leaving Leif to fade into the snow scene in his rear view mirror.

# three

STEPHEN'S VISIT WITH his Aunt Ellie is getting old, like the last piece of blueberry pie he's having for breakfast. Ellie is still at the post office when he dials Hawk's number. This time the guy he spoke with before answers the phone.

"He's not here," he tells Stephen. "He went to meet you at the fish houses. On Saturday."

Stephen feels his face go clammy. Did he forget? No. He never heard anything about the fish house on Saturday. He's sure. Never heard about any time or specific place.

"He never told me to meet him on Saturday."

"He left a message. You gave that number when you called before. He said nobody answered so he left a message. When somebody don't meet Hawk he gets mad. He don't like to wait for anyone. I think you'd better leave town, Mr. Spine."

"Damn. I didn't get any call about a meeting. Like I said, I have the money. All I've been doing is waiting to hear from Hawk."

"You better leave town," he says again and hangs up.

Stephen's hands are shaking. He sits down to eat the last bite of pie. He bites his tongue, drawing blood.

When Ellie returns he's in the bathroom holding a bloody washcloth on his tongue. She wants him to see a doctor, but no way is he going to let anyone near his mouth. Never has anything hurt so bad. Way worse than the time he slammed the car door on his finger that first year he started teaching and then a doctor made a small hole in his fingernail to relieve the

119

pressure. He thought he'd die. Now this is way worse. What did he do to deserve this? So what if he delivers drugs. So what if he buys black market sculpture. Why should he be afraid? Hawk actually does seem to like him. Maybe he does carve these beautiful works he buys. Maybe he's an angel in disguise. The drug money. He shudders. Oh hell, he mutters. I'm losing it.

"It's stopped bleeding. I don't need a doctor."

"Really, I think you'd better get it sewn up. I'm sure they would numb your tongue. Just like they do at the dentist," she tells him, like she's talking to a child.

He dabs at the tip of his tongue with a tissue.

"See, it's stopped bleeding." He lets his Aunt see the wound.

"Stephen, it's turning blue," she says in alarm.

"No, that's the blueberry pie," he says, thinking he'll never eat another piece of blueberry pie as long as he lives, which may not be too long. He'd better pack his bag. His tongue feels huge and swollen. He's certain that it's only going to get worse, and his speech is already clumsy. He tells his aunt he has to leave, that he has a few things to take care of in Duluth before he returns to Minneapolis. If it gets worse he can see his cousin's doctor. His Aunt makes him promise to see a doctor in Duluth, "even if it's better."

Stephen takes an aspirin and packs quickly and sloppily. Zipping up his case, he finds himself putting words in his head. "Hawk's gonna get ya," he says to himself, and then in the echo of his imagination he hears himself again, this time in the voice of James Cagney: "Hawk's gonna get ya." He hurries past the half-open closet door and out of the room.

*The laughter of a dark closet; the throbbing of blood within his tongue.*

The darn cute little dog with those big eyes looking at him like that, like he knows. God, a Chihuahua that knows all, sees all – why is he getting so paranoid, just when he was getting

120

better. Trouble of his own making. Biting his own tongue. Trying to shut up his own stupidity.

Aunt Ellie gives him a plastic bag with a wet washcloth and three of her arthritis tablets inside a tiny wooden box that says "Casino Winnings." Thank heavens he ate up the pie. If she had handed him a piece to bring along he would have been sick right there on the porch.

He hears James Cagney's voice again:

"Better get a move on, Stephen Spine. If you value your life."

His aunt stands out on the cold porch watching him drive away. She was crying when he said goodbye, but she smiled through her tears, the dear lady. She'll be back to her knitting after he leaves, knitting and pearling her dreams. He'll call her from Duluth and tell her he arrived. If he arrives.

How did he end up like this? Hearing voices – James Cagney, of all people. Like he's in some north woods Woody Allen film, of all things. Well, could be worse. He could be in some insipid western. He never liked westerns. Never liked John Wayne either. He's glad he's not hearing John Wayne's voice – better not even think about it. Don't tempt fate, like Jeannie used to say. And here he is, running from a man named Hawk. Maybe he'll never make it to Duluth. Maybe he'll end up in Moose Lake, or some home for the hopeless.

That black car behind him may be following him. Why does he have his lights on in the middle of the day? They can track people by phone numbers. They can track you anywhere. But Hawk drives a truck, doesn't he? Don't look in the mirror, just look at the road. Keep driving.

"Won't do you no good, you know that," says the James Cagney voice, now in the back seat of the car.

"Oh, shut up," Stephen says. He turns on the radio. "I'm in charge here," he adds, feeling much better with the radio on to keep him company, to keep him normal.

"California Dreamin" by The Mamas and The Papas comes on after the local news. The weather will be clear for the next two days, sunny and crisp. "On such a winter's day," Stephen sings along.

He's read about people like he's become. Paranoid, and then happy like this and singing along with The Mamas and The Papas without a care in the world.

"On such a winter's day," he sings all the louder. He always did have a pretty good singing voice. He's always liked to sing.

By the time he reaches Virginia, Stephen has forgotten about the black car. And this time he won't stop to visit Andrew. He won't even call. Of course they could meet for coffee somewhere. He knows he needs to confide in someone, and after all, he and Andrew have been friends for ages. But Andrew couldn't begin to understand, even though he would listen and he would truly care. Still, their friendship would never be the same. Andrew would advise him to see a priest or a psychiatrist, or both. Then he would start calling Stephen, and sending friendly little e-mail messages, just to see how he's doing. And what if he actually called the police? No, Virginia is not the place to stop.

At a gas station near Duluth, he fills up. Gas is ridiculously high. Someday he's going to get one of those electric cars, or one of those hybrids. Maybe a Toyota Prius. You can count on a Toyota. His old Toyota is the best car he's ever owned. Nothing ever goes wrong with it, while his colleagues are forever sitting in their mechanic's dreary little office or car dealership waiting for their expensive cars to be repaired. They get too attached to their fancy lemons.

Stephen sticks his tongue out in front of the grimy restroom mirror. It's still blue but not like it's black and blue, though it has raw looking edges. "Geez" he says, slamming the restroom door behind him, determined not to look again for the rest of the day. He buys a Reese's peanut butter cup and drives on, letting the candy melt on the good side of his mouth.

It's dark by the time he gets to Duluth. The red radio and TV tower lights above Twin Ponds are his favorite city lights. They stand in a row on the hill like a series of Eiffel towers with their cheerful red lights. There are more than a dozen towers now but when he was a kid there were just three and they were just as beautiful then, up above the hills where they had grass fires. Down below, the lights of the aerial bridge make him feel at home, as usual, even if he no longer lives in Duluth. Stephen wonders about the old guy he met by the bridge before he went to Ely. Surely he's home by now. He is someone Stephen could have talked to and perhaps even told about the Madonnas. Well, maybe not. Though he had probably heard it all, heard stranger stories by far. Tough losing a brother like that. Losing anyone.

He decides to drive down High Street to see if any lights are on at Sarah's. It's one of the steepest streets in town and he always takes it slow. A police car is in the driveway. What? He drives by at a snail's pace but can see no one through the front window. But that is definitely a police car. This is getting to be a bad day, and he doesn't exactly bite his swollen tongue, just nicks it with the edge of a tooth, enough to make it sting. He'll definitely take one of his aunt's pain pills when he gets to his cousin's. Funny, he's never even considered looking into those bags of drugs. Just didn't want to know, as if he personally would have nothing to do with drug running as long as he doesn't look. Dumb fool. He hears the words, but not in Cagney's voice this time.

BACK IN DULUTH

"HEY, JIM. What's up?"

"Oh, hi Steve," Jim says, smoothing out the nonexistent hair atop his head. "Nothing good on TV tonight. Guess I fell asleep. Want a beer?"

"Sure." Stephen takes his bag upstairs "I'll be down in a minute."

"On the counter," Jim yells up the stairs. "I'm going to bed. And someone called and left a message. From Morgan. Number's by the phone."

After Stephen showers, he puts on his old flannel robe that he leaves at Jim's. Down in the kitchen he takes a pill with a swig of beer. Both his tongue and his head are throbbing. He doesn't know why he is standing there staring at the phone number. He can't make himself call. He can't handle any bad news. He can hardly handle any good news today. Jeannie would just go ahead and dial. Find out right away. She would offer to help in any way she could. She was always helping people. Never hesitated. She would step right in, bringing someone a cake or pie, or pick up a book at the library, or a film for a bedridden friend. She knew just when someone needed a hug, or when they needed someone to sit and listen. Whatever it was, she knew just what to do.

Stephen pours the rest of his beer into a glass and dials Morgan's number.

# *four*

SARAH USES A CASINO DOLLAR coin to break the pain pill in half. She drinks half a cup of Coke to nudge the rough-edged pill down her throat. They keep bringing her free Cokes, ever since she sat down at the Go Fish slot machine. She never even liked Coke, but today finds it soothing and delicious in the smoky casino. She feels at home sitting on a stool in front of the Go Fish slot machine with its friendly fishermen and her own free glass of Coke. Though she knows it's foolish, she likes free things. Since marrying Morgan she has had no concern with money at all, unlike many of her friends. And now she has a fascination with Craigslist free items. Free stuff just gives her a thrill.

It doesn't feel at all like this is her first time in a casino. It's so easy. Just as easy as taking the wrong bus, which as it turned out, was the right bus. Yes, she could have taken the bus home, and that had been her intention. After perusing the downtown library shelves she was pleased with her little volume of Robert Frost poems. But she was restless, and had enjoyed strolling along the covered skywalk that spanned the entire length of Superior Street. As she walked along the glass walkway above Superior Street she could see the lake and the bridge, the old brick buildings that lined Superior Street and a few ships wintering over in the bay. Below on the sidewalk a few hardy souls were out walking, their shoulders hunched against the cold.

Sarah's back was sore by the time she reached the exit near Global Village, but as long as she kept herself distracted, the pain was tolerable. There was time to browse in the international store before going home, the store where she often shopped with Aunt Lilly. She lingered lazily at a table of brightly-colored scarves and shawls, running her fingers over an orange silk scarf, then a lime green shawl. She couldn't make up her mind. Then in the soap and candles she found a bar of Aunt Lilly's favorite lavender soap, and a fragrant cedar candle for Morgan, and a sandalwood candle for Tom Troll. She liked buying little presents, little surprises.

It was at the counter that she started to feel woozy, and as she looked at the rows of earrings reflected in the glass cabinet, the rows of jade and lapis and amethyst earrings began to double and triple themselves. When she laid her bills and coins on the counter top, the monkey, the Buddha statues, and the elephants on the near shelf seemed animated, especially their eyes, and the beaded curtain behind the clerk swayed and tinkled to the calming chant playing on the stereo system. At first she didn't hear what the clerk said, but some small new awakening came into her being and the next thing she knew she was out on Superior Street in the cold fresh air walking toward the bus stop. That was when she saw the Black Bear Casino bus sitting outside the Fond du Lac Casino, the small casino where Sears used to be. Tom Troll had told her you could now gamble in what used to be Sears old shoe department and you could play bingo up where they used to sell lamps. Both the Fond du Lac and Black Bear Casinos were owned by the Lake Superior Ojibwa.

She knew in an instant that she was going to take the bus to the Black Bear Casino instead of the bus to Lilly's house. Then on the Black Bear bus she sat with Jilly, a friendly, curly-haired woman around Aunt Lilly's age. Jilly laughed delightedly at everything, and when she found out Sarah had never gambled before, she told her how to play. She told Sarah what to look for and what to look out for. Her voice was loud and low, and the other passengers seemed to know Jilly and chimed in with their own advice on how to win at the Black Bear. The gentleman across the aisle agreed you could play a long time on the nickel slots, but she shouldn't get into a rut. She should branch out to the quarter machines and he recommended "The Wizard of Oz." Someone else told her to try "Go Fish," and a distinguished looking gentleman and the only man on the bus in a three-piece suit and tie, leaned around from his seat, pointed at her, and said simply "Volcano" before turning back to his newspaper.

Gathering her things together, she seems to be the last one to get off the bus. But no. There is someone in the very front seat slower than she is, a thin woman in a black coat still reading what appears to be a slim bible. She slams the book closed and stands up to follow Sarah out the door. "Bus of lost souls," she says. Sarah tells her they don't seem that lost and in fact they seemed happy and friendly. "Wait until the return trip," the thin woman says, and pulls her coat belt tight and takes off almost at a run toward the casino door.

Inside, Sarah gets right to it. It's quite easy and fun. She plays the Go Fish game and gets into the rhythm of punching the buttons and watching the screen. After she has no idea how long, she turns down an offer of a soda, and slides off her chair, already thinking of it as her chair, her lucky chair. Now, if she can find the bathroom in this confusing place. How noisy it is. While she was playing Go Fish she hadn't really noticed the noise of all the bells and cartoony toots and whistles emanating from the many rows of slot machines. As she walks along in search of the ladies' room, she notes how quiet the people are. If the electrical sounds were to be turned off, the casino would be a hall of silence.

Everyone in the row of dollar slots appears to be at least 80 years old. At the end of the aisle is the Bible woman. Where do they get the money? Passing a row of quarter machines she notes a woman playing three machines at the same time – the double diamond machine in front of her, plus a machine on either side. With a cigarette in her mouth she is pushing buttons on the three slot machines with an intensity Sarah has only previously seen on a cat ready to pounce. Why, is that Jilly? She isn't sure. So many people in the casino seem to look alike, or very similar, as though there are only a limited number of models available, something like cars. There are the Jilly-like women, with short curly brownish hair, and there are a lot of grandmotherly women with white hair, in both the smoker and nonsmoker models.

And she keeps seeing thin young men wearing plaid shirts. At first she thought it was the same guy, but in this row of slots near the bar alone she counts three. She'll call them the hippy lumberjacks. In college Sarah had a friend who categorized the students into the Greeks and the Granolas. She doesn't see many of those here.

"I'm probably a cross between a Jilly and a Granola," she muses as she pushes through the restroom door.

Coming out of her stall she sees Jessie at the mirror arranging her lavender hair. They hug, and Jessie says she's gone back to school and is studying Tarot cards on the computer. She plans to give readings in her husband's tattoo parlor, next door to the Shell station. Together they examine Sarah's blue braid and consider what to do now that her hair has grown out more than an inch since the blue was bonded on in the hospital.

"I think I'd like green," Sarah says.

"That's good. Green's a healing color. You could go two tone. Two strands of dark green and two lime. That'd be cool, Sarah. But don't cut off the blue. Let me unbond it when I do the green. Oh, I gotta go," she says, looking at her watch. "Call me any time." Jessie hands Sarah her card. "Any time. And good luck out there," she laughs and leaves Sarah to contemplate herself in the mirror.

She sees the puzzle of herself in the reflection from the mirror. There is a hint of her mother's face in her deep-set eyes, and something of her father in her nose, which seems larger, or somehow different since the accident, and she smiles, remembering Dr. Nose from the hospital. Those kindly people along the way seem almost like angels. Jessie certainly does. Now Jessie would be on the Granola side but still she's no Granola. She could be a Neon butterfly, Sarah decides, adding a new category and looking over Jessie's business card with a big hand-stamped butterfly over her name.

"So with my braid I'm a Jilly-Granola-Neon Butterfly," she says to herself, just as a Grandmother flushes and comes over to wash her hands. Sarah hopes she didn't hear her talking to herself.

"I just won a jackpot," the woman says, smiling.

"Congratulations!" Sarah tells her.

"It's all going for a deck. I've always wanted a deck where I can sit and watch the boats and the birds. In the summer I'll sit out there and drink my coffee and watch the birds. And I'll have a big pot of geraniums. Red ones. Oh, I'm so happy," she says, and tears start running down the woman's cheeks.

Sarah starts to cry too and can't think of a thing to say. The jackpot winner dabs at her eyes, straightens her shoulders and buttons her jacket.

"No, now, there don't you cry," she tells Sarah, patting her shoulder. "Your ship will come in one day too." As the soon-to-be owner of a deck is about to leave the restroom, she turns to wink, which makes Sarah laugh. Between the laughing and crying Sarah pulls herself together and decides she may just need something to eat and that her empty stomach is making her emotional. She'll have some nachos in the snack lounge.

Just outside the lounge she hears what sounds like beer caps in a blender. She recalls the jingle girl from the pow wow she went to with Morgan. Before the dancing began they sat behind a young lady whose mother was braiding her thick black hair. Sarah still remembers the beautiful hair ornament of aqua and white beads in a complicated diamond pattern, and the long silver earrings that hung gracefully below the angular curve of the young woman's cheek bones. After the braiding was finished, Sarah had taken pride in how lovely she looked, and had sensed that her own face wore the same expression as the mother's, even though she knew neither the mother nor the daughter. As the daughter walked off to the dance area, the gentle sound of the silver ornaments swaying against one another jingled like magical birds.

The Lady Slipper Lounge is mostly deserted. Sarah takes her nachos to the table furthest from the two hippie lumberjacks, one at either end of the bar – they always seem to be alone, at least here in the casino.

The one in the red plaid shirt saunters toward Sarah carrying two beers. Without looking at her he sets them down at the table next to Sarah and sits down with a sigh. Out of the corner of her eye she watches him position the two glasses, moving them numerous times until apparently they are satisfactorily positioned.

"Hawk," he calls out to the other guy at the bar. Hawk turns and Sarah can see he's no hippie lumberjack. She doesn't know what he is, and doesn't want to know. He shakes his head and turns back to his beer at the bar.

"Ah, shit," he says. He cocks his head and says to his beer, but really to Sarah, that Hawk's no fun, and where'd she get that blue hair?

Sarah is silent, trying to decide what she should do, if anything. Hawk stands abruptly and walks off, slipping on a black leather jacket.

"Whew. Some guy, hey?" he says, watching Hawk leave without a word. "I just met him at the bar. He's not my brother or anything. He likes Johnny Cash, and trouble, I think. You know how some people are just looking for it, kind of like inviting it on. But I always try to see the best in anyone. Little hard there, in his case, but then we just talked maybe ten minutes, and I did most of the talking. I guess I got a big mouth," he laughs. "Slim. Pleased to meet you." He extends a hand.

As soon as Sarah shakes hands with Slim he moves himself and his beers over to her table, but she doesn't mind much, now that Hawk has gone. Slim is wearing a small pink plastic pin in the shape of a bow on the collar of his shirt and now that he is right in front of her she can see that he has no teeth and no lips to speak of. His speech is clear enough, though perhaps a bit on the lispy side. Still, she can understand him just fine.

"Want a beer?"

"No thanks," she says, since she already has a Coke, not that she would accept his offer anyway.

"Good beer," he says with a slurp. They serve a good soup too. Wild rice with real wild rice – you know that pale brown kind. But I just had popcorn. Want to see my son-in-law's new truck? Ford pickup right out in the parking lot. Pretty blue."

"No thanks," Sarah says again, worried that she may have hurt his feelings and also wondering if she's giving the wrong impression, sitting with him.

"Anyway, there's a bear out there. A bunch of us were out looking at it and eating popcorn. I'm not afraid of bears. You afraid?" Sarah tells him, yes, she is afraid. They both sip their drinks at the same time.

"Know my real name?" he asks.

"No," Sarah says, surprised, since he's already said his name is Slim.

"Donovan Anderson."

"Fancy name," Sarah says.

"My folks couldn't think up a name for me so they let my sister name me. She picked Donovan."

"I'm Sarah," she says, preferring to remain somewhat vague. If he's a talker she can more or less relax and just listen. He tells her he's from Virginia and doesn't come to Duluth much anymore, that he and his wife Debbie used to come down every weekend for her radiation and chemotherapy at St. Mary's but now she's buried back home. "Damn cancer," he says, giving his beer glass a hard little whack with a spoon. Sarah tells him she's sorry. And she is too, even though she doesn't really know Donovan and never met his wife.

"You don't have a choice, that's the thing. What comes, comes. Before Virginia, we lived ten years in Silver Bay. My daughter says it was the water, all the taconite tailings pouring into the lake all those years and us drinking it. Jessica, that's my daughter, she's a beautician, and Rolf, my son-in-law with the truck – he sells smoked fish. And does tattoos. Says that's his art. He thinks everybody has to express themselves. Me, I talk. Guess that's my art."

So this is Jessie's father-in-law. She relaxes a bit, and muses that her art is probably yoga, though she knows there's something else for her, something she has yet to discover. Jessie is probably right about the asbestos in the water. She shudders, considering that she too grew up drinking Lake Superior water. She remembers seeing a map of concentrations of cancer deaths in the United States, and a dark shaded area near Lake Superior. It took a lawsuit to get Reserve Mining to stop pouring taconite tailings into the lake, and that suit dragged on and on.

They both drink in silence, and finally Sarah pushes her glass away and gets up, saying that she's going to give it a last try. "See if I have any luck," she says. He picks up his glass in a peculiar manner raising it about an inch above the table with both hands, as a kind of northland toast. She doesn't really know what he means by it, but feels honored by the gesture, and connected to him now that he's told her about his wife.

She's very tired, and her back aches nearly as much as it did when she was in the hospital. She takes the stairs to a landing with a window and looks out over the parking lot. No bears, only cars and it's already dark and beginning to snow.

Back on the main floor of the casino she walks along the nearest row of penny machines, looking for an empty seat, but they are all occupied. She stands near a corner machine. Might as well hang around and see if anyone is about to leave, but all the machines are occupied by people who look like they have no intention of leaving for a good long while. In fact they look so at home it makes her wonder if this is their home. And even though her back hurts, Sarah is feeling at home here too, even though Morgan forgot to buy her a hat. She'll call him, pretty soon. Probably. Funny that she just now thought of him.

At the end of the aisle a few of the machines have two players, one person playing and the other standing behind and looking on, as a consultant, or cheering squad. Probably the consultant is just out of money. On one side of the row, one man and three women are smoking. Down at the end machine a skinny girl in a fringed leather jacket is chewing gum. There is only one smoker on that side, plus three middle-aged women with short curly brown hair who all look alike. Definitely Jillies. The smoker is a fat guy whose stomach rests against the machine and wobbles each time he pulls the lever. A young hippie lumberjack with greasy black hair, drinking a beer, is watching the fat guy, like she is. What if Sarah knows all of these people? What if they were all in seventh grade together and all look so different now that they don't even know one another. Maybe the fat guy was an old friend from her high school band, now so altered by pizza and beer that whoever he is, or was, has been buried beyond recognition.

Maybe amnesia is something like this. All of the five cent gamblers are playing with that concentration she keeps seeing, pushing buttons and pulling levers as though mesmerized or hypnotized, like there is a zombie inside each of the gamblers. She feels it within herself and realizes it happened about one minute after she stepped inside the casino door. How amazing that you can be so peaceful in such a place and completely forget where you are and what time it is or even what season it is, and that you actually have something to do the next day and maybe people are wondering where you are. But her regular life seems far off, like part of some other lifetime. Maybe she'll just always live here in the casino and never even need to sleep.

It feels good, how her normal self has disappeared and this other, more peculiar self, this freer self, is wandering around the casino. What she doesn't mind is that she can be any way she likes; she's not committed to being her usual self at all and there is something refreshing about that, even if there is a bit of the zombie in it. Perhaps this is what Morgan finds, living in the jungle.

———————

NOW WHAT'S THAT? A six-foot tall yellow half moon is walking toward Sarah, wearing a money hat with tiny twinkling lights and carrying a big golden basket. The moon seems to be made of a rubbery material like the rubber ducks kids use in the tub, but not as bright a yellow. You can buy a chance at Moonlight Money from him for two quarters, plus you get free coupons. The drawing, which is for ten thousand dollars, takes place at midnight. Sarah knows this because they announce it every half hour. She overheard someone telling how last month it was Comet Cash, and the guy caught on fire but someone saved him with a large Coke.

Sarah decides to buy a chance. Apparently most people have their tickets by now because she is the first person in line and only two people line up behind her.

"Thank you," Sarah says to the moon, which disorients her a bit and she gets flustered writing her name on the ticket with the stubby pencil covered with tooth marks but all the same she does it and slides the ticket into the slot of the Moon's metal box. She gets a packet of coupons and steps over near the wall to see what she received from the moon:

50 cents off a Pipe Dream Ice Cream, individual size
2 for 1 oil change, Lakeshore Viking
Half off price one large Pizza Puff
2 Free Bingo cards, good Sunday only
May 17 Lefse Festival pass, Lake Superior Lutheran basement, 1 to 4 p.m.
1 Mosquito Magic, 1 oz. pocket size.

Not too bad, and anyway, it doesn't hurt to try. A pizza puff sounds good, whatever it is, which is probably nice and cheesy with air bubbles like you get on a crust sometimes, only this would be a really big one, with extra crispy cheese, like the overflow of a cheese volcano. Too bad they only sell them downtown, whatever they are. She folds her coupons and ticket stub and spots an empty seat at a Black Widow quarter machine at the nearby row of slots.

Forgetting about the moon, and Morgan, she unrolls her last roll of quarters. It goes pretty well at first, and she spins to a cluster of cherries three times in row, winning six quarters each time. Next she spins several nothings in a row, and finally, two Black Widows. She waits to see what she's won, but apparently she has won nothing. Indeed, the chart on the machine indicates that two spiders win nothing. You need three spiders to win, which doesn't seem fair, as she has always liked spiders, and after all, she had a black widow living in her sweet peas all one summer. It would come running to investigate when it felt water droplets on its web from the sprinkling can. How beautiful it was, all black and glossy as patent leather and round as a marble, with long capable legs and a perfect red hourglass on its underbelly. Surprisingly, its web was neither neat nor beautiful. Morgan told her that if you encounter such a formless web, you can tell if it's a black widow's by testing its strength. A widow's web will hold a penny without breaking. Oh well. She leaves the machine.

Sarah's feet feel heavy, like she's sinking into the floor a bit, perhaps just an inch or two, and her mouth is dry from all the smoke in the casino. She needs another Coke, but stops to watch a woman wearing a red sweat shirt with a loon on its back. The gentlemen on either side of her seem quite happy sitting next to this pretty, winning grandmother, and they regularly pause to watch her game as she racks up one win after another. They are all playing Treasure Island. Sarah watches the revolving pictures, and feels the parrots are spinning in her eyes and that she has become part slot machine. Three pirates look like the three identical brown-haired Jillies from the other side, only with hats and eye patches. The men on either side of the grandmother are working hard now, pushing buttons and pulling levers like they are captains of a pirate ship, steering a true course to keep everyone from capsizing. The little swashbuckling group is huddled together like a right friendly silent crew, and Sarah feels a part of it too. "Welcome to Fantasy Island." Now who said that? It must have been from another machine. Unless she's starting to hear voices again, like back in the hospital.

After a few minutes she rubs the back of her head and yawns. She wanders off past the dollar machines and the Black Jack tables to watch the fish in the big tank near the door. Morgan is building an aquarium in their new house on Park Point, where they'll have beautiful golden fish. These trout are elegant and sleek and some have stripes the color of dragonflies, and others, spots like opals. The bass are fat and gray. She watches the biggest bass as it opens and closes its mouth with exaggerated precision. It seems to be sounding out words phonetically. Sarah tries to read its lips, and feels sorry it can't get out and go back to its lake. The fish look old and she wonders if these fish used to be gamblers, and somehow got turned into fish. The bass looks straight at Sarah, then swims off into the dark swishy weeds.

Bells start ringing behind Sarah. She hurries over to see where the excitement is coming from. It's a dollar machine with lights blinking where an old man has just won $2,000. He's standing beside his machine waiting for the attendant. His hair is white and he's wearing a dazzlingly white shirt. He's tall and lean and there's a formal air about him. Also, he looks like he's about to cry. In fact, Sarah thinks she has never seen a man look so sad. Maybe he knows he's going to turn into a fish.

She leans against the coffee bar and all the noise and people start to blend into one almost indecipherable picture and the rows of slot machines appear to be sliding, the colors and numbers running off onto the floor, oozing and melting like Dali's melting clocks. Donovan walks up to her and smiles. He's put his teeth in.

"Moon magic," he says and points down the hall. She watches people crowd around a little red curtain on the far side of the casino and makes her way toward the group. A drum roll begins and bells ring like it's a fire station and the lights start flashing. Sarah fidgets with her coupons and the ticket stub inside her pocket, and starts to breathe in little jerky breaths.

LADIES AND GENTLEMEN!
Ten T-H-O-U-S-A-N-D DOLLARS
of MOON MONEY MAD MAD MAD MADNESS, goes to –
Donovan Anderson!

Sarah hears a woman squeal somewhere and she feels like squealing herself. People are jumping. She feels on fire with excitement. Not until Frank Sinatra starts singing *Fly me to the Moon*, does she realize she is all alone and hasn't even called Morgan to tell him where she is, and now it must be midnight. At the phone, she hesitates for a moment, listening to the music . . . *to Jupiter and Mars . . ..*

"Morgan?"

———  ——  ——

DRIVING AWAY FROM THE bright lights of the casino she looks out the window into the black night, happy to be going home with Morgan. She hasn't turned into a fish, or worse and even though she didn't win, she feels like a winner. She feels renewed, and peaceful.

Sarah falls asleep as soon as they pull out of the Black Bear parking lot. When Morgan arrived at the casino he found her staring into a tank of native fish, eye to eye with a big-mouthed bass. He had never seen her so tired, yet she seemed relaxed and happy to see him, as if she had experienced a mystical revelation. It gave him a hopeful feeling about their future. But it had been a hell of a night, and he's glad it's over and she's safe. He'll tell her about Sam Light in the morning.

*Sam, Sam, the Piper's son.*
*Stole a Pig and away he run.*

Lulu surprised him when she recited that old rhyme, changing the name to fit the thief. She was a great help all through the evening. You just never know who is going to have their feet on the ground in a crisis. What a shock, though, calling the police to see if they had any news about Sarah, and instead hearing that Sam Light had been picked up at Toby's coffee shop in Hinkley, halfway to the Twin Cities, with a trunk full of drug paraphernalia, huge amounts of cocaine hidden in a fishing tackle box, Lilly's laptop and gold jewelry. He even stole her Buddha with the cross, all wrapped in the antique Persian carpet from the hall. What a rat. He should have trusted his own instincts early on.

Grateful to have Sarah back, Morgan can't think of a longer day since she was in the hospital. He knew he wasn't thinking clearly when he kept driving back up to Chester Park and down again, a good seven times, maybe more. After each drive he would call the police and the hospitals, try the people on his list, then heat water for tea and leave after barely taking a sip. He knew he was acting similar to smokers who light a cigarette while they already have one going, hands shaking all the while.

Lulu spent the evening scouring the stove, one stainless-steel burner at a time. He is not having that kind of stove on Park Point. They'll have a six-burner gas stove. He and Lulu had been quiet for much of the evening, when he wasn't driving, imagining the worst for Sarah and trying not to. That was probably why he kept driving to Chester - that image of Sarah in the snow, the bloody snow, was making him crazy. What a horrid night. My God, what if she hadn't called.

Sarah stirs in her seat and straightens up with a stretch.

"Morgan, I'd like to see our house on Park Point tomorrow. If I can wake up. Probably I'll sleep until noon. Oh, here," she yawns, digging in her purse. "I brought you a candle." She rests the sandalwood candle on top of her purse.

"Good. We'll see the house tomorrow. I had some photos developed, but it's best you see for yourself." Except for the tower, from here on, it's all inside work. He's thrilled with her renewed interest in the house and decides not to tell her that the maple floor in the meditation and yoga room is finished. He's anxious to see her reaction when she stands in the room and looks out through the glass wall to the panoramic view of Lake Superior. He's glad he never told Sam about the yoga room.

She'll be shocked when he tells her about Sam the thief. He doubts she'll say much. He resolves to talk things over more with her. They are each taciturn by nature, and sometimes that's good. But this whole hell of an evening wouldn't have happened if they talked more, perhaps. Who knows? Sam did help her with her recovery, he'll give him that.

He spots a group of deer in the ditch ahead and slows down. The deer walk single file along the side of the road, flicking their tails, taking their time.

"Why are their eyes so noticeable at night like that?" Sarah asks.

"They have a reflective material at the back of their eyes," he says.

"Our eyes should shine like that when we're out walking along the road. Why don't people have that reflecting thing?"

"Maybe we used to. I don't know. I don't know everything," Morgan says, feeling that he knows nothing at all on this night in the northland. But he plans to learn.

The lights of Duluth come into view as they crest the rise of a hill, and the familiar lights flow over the hills like a brilliant reflection of the Milky Way. The familiar bridges are lit like low constellations, with the bridge connecting Duluth and Superior marking its length across the long expanse of the St. Louis River like a long string of diamonds. The great aerial bridge with its arch of shimmering silver light welcomes them home in the silence of the night.

# five

STEPHEN WAKES IN A COLD SWEAT. He gets out the Hudson Bay blanket from the closet and climbs back into bed, trying to warm up, but he can't stop shivering. He gets up again to turn up the thermostat, which surprisingly, has already been turned up to where he likes it, just on the high side of 70, and he can hear that it's on. The curtains beside the bed are fluttering above the heating vents. Still, he is freezing. He sees blood on the pillow case, and with a sinking feeling of dread, turns on the light and gets up to look at his tongue in the mirror. It looks bad, but not any worse than this afternoon.

How odd, that call with Morgan. He sure is a strange one, telling Stephen that Sarah isn't there and everything is fine, when it's 11:00 o'clock at night and there's a police car in the driveway.

*"Who are you calling strange? You look pretty strange yourself in that Indian blanket."*

It's the James Cagney voice again. Stephen decides to ignore it. He'll call Gigi. She's called him in the middle of the night before. Just hearing her voice should help. It's the voices of women he falls for. They tell him everything. He's helpless around certain voices. It's ringing. He must be tired because he forgot that Jeep might answer. Luckily, Gigi answers and tells him that Jeep is out of town and suggests that he come over. "You're not yourself, Stephen," she says.

He sneaks out of the house as quietly as he can, dressed warmly so the shivering doesn't start up. He borrows Jim's big

Russian fur hat that he gave him two Christmases ago. He has to remove the tissue stuffing from the hat before he can put it on. He vows to buy Jim nothing but boxes of candy from now, something he'll use, or at least eat.

Gigi opens her porch door before he knocks. She's dressed in a red velvet robe and takes his hand and leads him inside and down the hallway of masks.

"Meow," Gigi says looking coyly over her shoulder at Stephen.

They kiss beneath the large chandelier and for one second Stephen feels outright bliss, just before he yowls out in pain.

"What?

"My tongue," he says, holding his hand over his mouth.

He follows her to an overstuffed green couch in the living room and sits down, watching her light the fire. She pours them each a glass of Drambuie and Stephen tells Gigi how he bit his tongue in Ely this morning and about the blueberry pie. He tells her about Hawk, about the police car at Sarah's, about his garden, his converted coal bin and he even tells her about the Madonnas. He tells her absolutely everything, except for his new friend, James Cagney. They sip and clink their little aqua-rimmed Mexican glasses in sleepy toasts. By the time the sky begins to lighten, they're high and mighty friends, just as they were once before.

In the morning Gigi gets the answering machine when she calls for Sarah. She has half a mind to tell her she's heard Morgan is stepping out on her. She and Sarah were good friends once, and she owes her that. Sarah was always the smart one. She probably knows. No, she won't say anything, just wants to know if she's okay.

Maybe the police car didn't mean anything bad. Once her Dad helped push a Santa Claus out of a snow drift in front of their house at Christmas. The Santa was an off duty cop on his way to a party and the snow was blinding that night, at least according to the stories she was later told. Of course he just may have been boozing. After they got the car shoveled out he came into her room in his fine red suit and whispered her name. She awoke to a red-faced Santa handing her a big beautiful doll and wishing her a Merry Christmas. It was a doll with red curls and a pink dress and bonnet that she came to love. That Santa made her a believer long after her friends had given up on him. So maybe the police car in Sarah's drive was stuck. There may be some perfectly innocent explanation.

She really wants to talk to Sarah about Stephen. She might have some ideas about how to help. There's no reason she can't be a confidant with both Stephen and Sarah. But Stephen definitely needs help, the way he was talking and answering someone who wasn't there toward morning. Well, they had each drunk too much, that's for sure. Maybe Stephen just has a temporary mental imbalance, due to stress during the holidays. And where is Sarah? She calls again and this time leaves a message on the machine. "It'll all come out in the wash," she says. That's what Gigi's mother used to say.

Stephen heads for the kitchen when he smells Gigi's coffee.

"Mmmm." He says. "My cousin makes horrible coffee."

Gigi is alarmed at Stephen's swollen cheeks and the skin above his mouth and half his nose puffed out and his lips are taut and shiny pink, looking like they're ready to explode.

"Morning Stephen," she says, forcing a smile. "How do you feel this morning?"

"You know, it's funny. I feel just like hell and my head feels like it's stuffed with socks. But I feel fantastic. Like a new man!"

Gigi hands him a cup of coffee and sits down at the table with her mug. Ordinarily she would come right out and say his breath smelled like rats, if it did, and which it does, but not this morning.

"It's stopped snowing," Stephen says, wiping his chin of dribbled coffee. "This is wonderful coffee, Gigi." She tells him it's Peace coffee and that it was Sarah's Aunt Lilly who recommended it, that day she served chai and coffee on the day of Sarah's homecoming party.

They sip coffee and look out on the peaceful white lake. The sunrise is beginning to brighten the ice. Gigi pops a sugar lump into her mouth and sucks her coffee through the sugar, as is her habit while watching the morning sky over Lake Superior. Stephen thinks she should be an actress, the way a person can see in her face whatever she's feeling and he knows what men want from Gigi – some of that ecstasy. He sees it right there as she sucks in the morning sunrise through her coffee-drenched sugar cube. It's almost like too much pleasure has been allotted to this one person.

Gigi asks if he ever thinks of moving back to Duluth. "Oh, sometimes," he says. He had been thinking about that just before Christmas. Not too seriously, but still he was thinking about it. But of course if Hawk is out to kill him, the further away he is, the safer he'll be. "Hawk may really be after me."

"Is he smart? Could he find you, do you think? Through your books, or the college? Does he have your address?"

"He's smart all right. He always wanted cash. He wouldn't take a check. I don't think he has my address, but I'm right there in the phone book. He pilots a big boat on the Lake, so he probably knows computers. Probably he'll find me."

"I don't know. I think he'll be trying to find you just to get the money. Make the deal. You can move here, Stephen," Gigi says, laughing for the first time all morning. "Could you have given him the wrong number and then he left the message about meeting him on someone else's answering machine?"

"Oh Lord. The way things have been going. I could have. I could have done that." He hasn't been himself this week. He hasn't been himself since Jeannie died. Maybe he's never been himself.

Gigi sets out yogurt for them both, and pours more coffee. Stephen finishes the smooth yogurt carefully. He hasn't been able to eat much since he bit his tongue and this vanilla yogurt is delicious and creamy. He knows he'll have to see a doctor today, there's no getting around that. The healing is just not going right. What if Sarah is sick again and they both end up in the hospital. But then it would have been an ambulance, not a police car in front of her house. Unless she was in an accident elsewhere. Out in the bad weather. They never did find the driver of the car that hit Sarah. Maybe Tom Troll was visiting Sarah and Morgan. The cop may have spotted his taxidermy truck in front of the house and stopped to report a moose accident and someone needing the moose head prepared for their media room. Stephen laughs at himself. Could be he has a fever.

"What?" Gigi laughs too, thinking he doesn't seem crazy this morning.

"I was thinking about Tom Troll, the taxidermist. I met him at Sarah's."

"Yes, me too. At Sarah's party. I thought he was shy. Very quiet. He likes to polka."

"Polka?"

"There was dancing at the homecoming party? Now that seems not quite appropriate, with Sarah so ill."

"Well, she fell asleep. We were all dancing, except Morgan and Sarah. Morgan played the piano and Julia sang and this skinny guy, Leif something, played the accordion. He was really good – very musical."

Gigi stands beside the large kitchen window facing the lake. "Sometimes it seems like it's been white out there forever. Like spring will never come," she says.

# *six*

---

"TRANSFORMATION OF THE MIND. That's what Aunt Lilly has written here on the first page of her dictionary," Sarah says, sitting cross-legged on Lilly's bed with the Duluth News Tribune crossword puzzle on her lap. Morgan sits down beside her.

"You used to sit like this," he says, amazed at her agility this morning.

"I know. Isn't it strange? My whole body feels different. Almost normal," she says. The puzzle is hard this morning and she's enjoying the dictionary more than the puzzle. On the same page of the dictionary she notes Gracie Allen, Woody Allen, and an alligator. "Gracie Allen," she reads: 'American comedienne best remembered for the confused but unflappable foil to her husband and stage partner, George Burns." Such interesting facts. "Alligator was what I was looking up. They have the shorter nose and the crocodiles have the long skinny ones. Oh you know that – how funny, me telling you about nature. See, here on page 48."

He leans close. The Woody Allen photo was taken in 1987. He finds the alligator drawing to be inadequate. Morgan wants to hold Sarah, but he is afraid she is still too fragile. He strokes her arm. He's had close calls with both alligators and crocs. He wants to keep her from harm, from crocodiles, from Carmen, from the knowledge of Sam Light's crimes.

"Well, I think we should go see the house. If we get there before 10:00 we'll have the house to ourselves. Ted is coming some time after 10:00 to set tile."

Sarah smiles contentedly at Morgan.

"You seem quite unflappable today, Sarah," he says.

She smiles at Morgan again. She wants to see the house, but first asks if he saw all the phone messages on the answering machine from last night.

"They can wait," Morgan tells her. "I listened last night. I woke up a couple of times and listened while I finished the Ben & Jerry's vanilla."

"If you get fat, beautiful women will stop chasing you." She hasn't told him that Carmen stopped by the house the other day and they had tea. What a strange brassy scientist woman, Sarah had thought. Carmen was careful to portray her friendship with Morgan as purely academic, but Sarah knew right away. She knew how her husband affected women. Even her friend Gigi was flirting with Morgan right there in front of her at her hospital homecoming party. She doesn't know why, but she's always been confident about herself with Morgan. People comment on her beauty, but she takes it lightly. The only woman she has ever been truly jealous of was Morgan's mother, before she died. She was a grand lady who loved Morgan dearly but basically ignored him in favor of her charity work. Sarah has always wondered if it's true, that men marry a woman like their mother; that he likes her because she ignores him and is generally indifferent to his compliments. Still, she cares for him. Or does she?

She'll consider talking to Morgan about Carmen. They should start talking to each other more than they have in the past. Sarah takes care with her hair, quickly tying her blue braid with a strand of tiny blue beads. She's looking forward to seeing the house. Also, she would like to play Go Fish again.

---

THE HOUSE ON PARK POINT is set back from the road and framed by tall pines, which extend out onto both sides of the house, giving the property a private and park-like appearance. As you near the house you see that it's set in the middle of rolling sand dunes which slope down to the beach, which is part of the five-mile sand peninsula of Park Point, officially known as Minnesota Point.

It is a sunny day and unusually warm for January. Morgan and Sarah walk from room to room in the morning sunlight. Morgan runs his fingers through the dust on the piano in the grand room of the main floor. The Steinway sits on one of Sarah's favorite Persian carpets from his parents' estate.

"You've been busy, getting all this done," Sarah exclaims. The sunlight flowing over the big room makes her feel like dancing and she prances across the floor like a ballerina, stopping before the George Morrison wood collage she so adores. "Just perfect!" she says. She never tires of the Morrison piece. And it has never looked as good as now, on this wall of their almost-finished Park Point home. She sees it in a new way each time she stands before it, her old wooden friend. Pieces of driftwood are fashioned into an abstract landscape of land and sea, with straight pieces and curved pieces, all weather worn to a soft silvery gray. A paler wooden circle like a moon completes the work. Sarah sighs.

The main floor bath is like it was the first time she saw it. Neither she nor Morgan had wanted to change a thing. It was a little shrine of perfection right down to the last detail. It was blue and gray. The stone work was gray and the tiles a lake blue. A design of long curving blue mosaic spread above the bath and shower, with accents of gold and shimmering amethyst. They hadn't been able to find out who did the exquisite mosaic work. Someone had thought it was done by an art student who visited from Italy one summer, but didn't know the person's name.

Down a few stairs is the sauna and hot tub, which they designed together. Above the tub a stained-glass window filters the light through lavender and white water lilies floating in a sea of blue. She loves the rich colors and fine craftsmanship and excellence of the design, and imagines soaking in a tub of bubbles, contemplating the beauty of the Tiffany window, one of their very few concessions to luxury and an acknowledgement of Morgan's wealth.

When they were looking for a house shortly before they were married, Morgan wouldn't even consider looking at a house if it were brick. Brick walls and hedges he could not abide, saying he associated them with the mausoleum where he grew up. That cold dark house, he called it.

Their footsteps echo throughout the empty house as they climb to the second floor. Morgan takes great pride showing Sarah how the fish tank is shaping up in the upstairs shower. They'll be the first ones to shower in this shower with the view, he has mentioned several times. One night he told Lilly that he thought it would be like a baptism, to be the first to shower where no one has showered before. Sarah had laughed at his Star Trek comment. "Where no one has ever showered before," she says dramatically, sticking her head into the shower enclosure. Morgan leans near and looks at her, as if they are ready to kiss, but they only stare at one another in wonder. Both are without words.

Upstairs, the bedroom looks out onto the lake and they look out in silence. Sarah moves near Morgan and runs her arm along his. As they embrace she sees the scarf, a women's beige scarf lying on top of one of the boxes of tile. It's not hers. She backs away and picks up the scarf and a little devil of a worm stirs inside her – a little hate worm, a little worm of jealously. She feels it inflate with her breath.

"Carmen's, I suppose," she says accusingly, holding out the scarf.

Morgan is dumbstruck, but walks blindly toward Sarah, through the wall suddenly grown between them. Sarah backs away.

"She's gone. She was here, but she's gone."

"She isn't gone, Morgan. She came to see me. I talked to her."

Morgan sits down on the box of tiles.

"Oh hell. Sarah, she follows me," he says.

"Morgan, how can you be so smart and then be so dumb." She throws the scarf at Morgan. It flutters between them like a silky dying moth.

"These stupid women," Sarah says, beginning to pace. "Stupid stupid women. Red-headed stupid women. Oh damn. Damn , damn. Guess I'll have to just kill her then. Then you can visit me in jail."

Morgan is shaken, and speechless.

Sarah leaves him sitting on the boxes and looks around the rest of the upstairs. His workroom looks unfinished but well used and she can see he's in the middle of a new book. Papers, notes and books are everywhere. One wall is covered with sticky notes, reminding her of the fly paper at her grandfather's farm of long ago. Photos of ferns and birds hang from a wire stretched across the room. His bird clock in the corner chirps out the hour. It's 10:00 o'clock, the hour of the chickadee. And time for the tile guy to arrive. Anyway, Carmen has fat tree trunk legs and a squeaky voice. She shudders, brushing Carmen off like an irritating bug.

The rest of the upstairs is nearly complete. Even in her state, she is thrilled with her yoga/meditation room. The small blue rug she loves is rolled up in the corner and the maple floor is finished. And the view! In spite of everything, she runs to sit beside Morgan on a box of tile to thank him for the wonderful yoga room.

"Oh, let's just forget it," she says. "Pretend we've just escaped from a Woody Allen movie." They sit quietly for a while, Morgan still speechless, realizing Sarah is more interested in the house than their relationship. Could that be true?

"Lilly says we need to look down on ourselves as if from the stars," Sarah says.

Downstairs the front door opens. It's time for Ted the tile guy to get to work. It's time for Morgan and Sarah to move on.

# part 3

SPRING

# *one*

SPRING ARRIVES AND LILLY returns from India. The smell of chai, incense, and fresh air fills the house. Lilly is home. She has opened the front windows and the lace curtains flutter in the breeze. In the backyard six bright saris hang in a row on the clothes line while at the base of the clothes poles, mounds of snow linger from the last storm of the year. A robin hunts for worms in the newly thawed sections of grass. In the air is the smell of spring and the sound of melting snow dripping and running down the street. Water trickles down the sidewalk, rushing and gurgling along the gutters of High Street.

A foghorn blows over the lake. Lilly stops to listen. She recites her sister's poem to the empty house:

To some a robin on the wing
May be a certain sign of spring
Or should a crocus raise its head
Above its cold and snowy bed
Yet the sound we wait so long to hear
A welcome nuisance to the ear
The moaning fog horn, that's the thing
That lets us know at last its spring.

How she does love Duluth in the spring! Lilly is looking forward to the Lefse Festival at the Lutheran church. She missed the past two years because she returned from Delhi a few days too late, not then ready to attend without Thor, her dear friend Pastor Thor Fjelstad.

Lilly smiles to herself, remembering the spring he brought her a bouquet of fresh red radishes. How they had laughed and then sat out on the back deck drinking ice water with mint and dipping radish slices in salt – just the way they liked them. Thor never had much time and was always on his way to a meeting or a consultation or some church work or one errand or another. She knew he spent a great deal of time on his sermons, and liked to take long walks at Chester Park in consideration.

Occasionally he would take time out and invite Lilly to his tiny retreat cabin just north of Duluth. She would stay with Thor's cousin, June, who had a larger cabin across the road and up the hill above her antique store. June also sold bears which her son carved from logs. Lilly, Thor, and June would sit out on the deck of Thor's cabin in the evenings and eat lefse. He had a good view of the lake from the deck, which was considerably larger than the tiny retreat cabin. June always left first, and that's when she and Thor could talk most freely.

Thor would recite whole sections of the Bible, beautiful or puzzling passages of his choosing, and they would discuss them while the sun set over the lake. With Lilly, Thor was free to express his doubts, his disappointments, his hopes and his fears, both large and small. As his illness progressed, he became quiet much of the time, and liked to have Lilly read poetry aloud. He liked Wordsworth and Frost, Rilke and Eliot. Once they sat outside the deck and listened to a tape of Allen Ginsberg reciting the poem, *Kaddish*. They had both been moved by the poem, by its musical rhythms, making itself into a song, and most of all they had been moved by his passion. Another time they listened to an old tape of The Shadow, until the little portable tape player got stuck on the Shadow's laughter. They made up an ending themselves. Thor had the books but sometimes Lilly would bring something along, and then he would do the reading. From Lilly's notebook of favorite poems, Thor chose one he had read before:

Konnie Ellis

The great sea has set me in motion,
Set me adrift,
Moving me like a weed in a river

The sky and the strong wind
Have moved the spirit inside me
Till I am carried away
Trembling with joy.
[Uvavnuk (Mid-19$^{th}$ – early 20$^{th}$ Century]

They had sat and rocked in the old glider chairs until it got dark. There were no bugs that night, and the sky changed from blue to lavender. When it turned crimson she began to chant softly. She remembers they could still hear the waves washing against the rocks down on the shore. Toward the end, Thor joined in the chant, something he had never done before, and their voices complimented one another with a perfection she knew she would never hear again, at least in this lifetime. Then, just as suddenly as she had begun, they both ended on the same note, and it was dark. They listened to the crickets for a minute or so and then she helped Thor carry the cups and saucers inside. Two days later she received a call from June telling her that Thor had died.

———

LILLY STANDS AT THE WINDOW. Here they come. Sarah drives in with Lulu. As they pull into the drive she can see that Lulu has dyed her hair that goldish blond color again. It reminds Lilly of a cat she once knew. She doesn't know why people dye their hair. To her all natural colors are beautiful. Yet she did like that blue braid Sarah had before she went to India.

"Yoo hoo. Here we are," Lulu says, bustling in. "It's wonderful having you back, Lilly." She gives her a hug. Sarah

157

joins in, then takes an end of Lilly's rose-colored sari, hanging on as a child might. "First fog horn of the year," she says, "just as we pulled in. I'm so glad you're back Lilly. It's been a long winter."

They all climb into Sarah's new car, ready for the Lefse Festival. Sarah dropped off their lefse last night. It was her first attempt at lefse making on her own, if she didn't count the practice batch from last week, and most of those were too thick, and either undercooked or burnt. She was surprised at her success this week. It was the loan of Aunt Lilly's lefse iron that helped, and she felt like a pioneer of sorts, cooking on that antique lefse iron, probably brought over from Norway.

As a child she had helped her mother rice potatoes. Then she would watch as her mother rolled out the lefse on the bread board, adding just the right amount of flour to keep them tender. Sarah was allowed to roll out a few small ones herself with bits of leftover dough. Today there'll be someone making lefse at the festival, and she intends to be a careful observer. The lefse table is always the most popular spot in the hall because they are so delicious and it brings people back to their mother's kitchens where they ate lefse right off the stove, soft and warm with butter and sugar.

Sarah finds a spot close to the church so they have only a half block to walk. As they stroll toward the church Lilly talks about the temples in India and how you have to take off your shoes before you enter and how they are so beautiful and smell of incense and flowers. They all know the incense of the Lutheran church is coffee, which wafts up from the basement hall as soon as they step indoors. Lilly recalls Thor describing the distinct aroma of Lutheran church coffee brewed in large quantities in the church basement, with an egg tossed in for clarity. He said it was a combination of the coffee, hymnals, and the perfume of old lutefisk and Swedish meatball dinners, particles of which had settled permanently into the structure of the building and were released by the steam of the large coffee pots.

There is a good crowd. The chatter of voices in the big hall is upbeat, yet with serious undertones in recognition of the location, even if it is a festival. Lulu sees Leif in the lefse line and hurries to greet him, happy that he has finished his spring cleaning at Chester Park in time to come to her church for lefse.

Sarah and Lilly watch a woman spin wool. She pulls the raw wool out of a birch basket, easing it through her fingers into a continuous strand of yarn, all the while keeping the wheel spinning with her foot. She tells them she also spins dog wool, though you can't use the hair of some short-haired dogs. She prefers poodle wool because of its similarity to sheep wool. She knits the spun dog wool into vests, and points out two vests made of poodle fur on her display table. "Right beside my business cards," she says. Both Lilly and Sarah take a card.

Lilly knows the woman demonstrating quilting at the next table. They watch as she makes precise stitches with a small needle on a quilt square of blue and lavender. Sarah takes one of her cards too. She and Morgan could use a quilt for the downstairs guestroom.

Under the big clock, June's son is painting the nose of a wooden bear. Some of the work he does with a power saw he explains, and says he did that last weekend, and now he's doing the touchy work. Apparently he has sold a number of bears. They saw someone leaving with a bear as they entered, and a few people are walking around the hall with a carved bear in their arms.

They watch a birdhouse maker and then a man who makes snowshoes. A woman, beautiful enough to be a model, is knitting a pair of black and white mittens. She has Norwegian sweaters and socks for display and sale on her table and Lilly buys a pair of slipper stockings.

"We still have cold evenings ahead," she tells the pretty woman, who seems as nice as she is pretty. Sarah buys a pair of mittens.

They spot Tom Troll at a table by himself near the back exit door, a poor location. Someone must have thought he would be doing something gruesome, placing him there, but he is busily painting the feet of a seagull, apparently content and oblivious to his isolated table. They watch for a while, chatting as he finishes a foot. Lilly invites Tom to dinner. He looks up at her with pleased amazement, and tells her he would be happy to join her for dinner. As an afterthought, he asks if he should bring white wine or red wine.

"A red would be nice," Lilly says, surprising both Sarah and herself, not only because it seems such a sophisticated thing for Tom to ask, but also because she is nearly always a teetotaler and of course a complete vegetarian, and here she is, inviting Tom Troll, the taxidermist, to dinner. Lilly smiles at the simple wonder and complexity of life.

Standing to one side of Tom's table, Sarah spots Stephen Spine and Carmen, looking comfortably cozy together.

"Well," she says. "I couldn't have predicted that."

"What, Sarah?" Lilly asks, joining her.

"Look, next to the flat bread and cheese table."

"Is that Stephen with --? Well, it is, isn't it. You just never know," Lilly says.

"Carmen. The redhead is Carmen," Sarah says.

"Do you know her, Sarah?"

"Unfortunately, I do."

"Then it seems everyone knows Carmen," Lilly says, concerned for Sarah. "Are you okay with this?"

"Oh, why not. But don't invite them to dinner – not when I'm around." They walk toward the lefse line.

---

THE FOLLOWING WEEK IS pleasantly warm and Lilly and Sarah are having tea on Lilly's back deck. They sit with their feet stretched out, basking under the sun and listening to the birds chatter in the trees of the creek. Both agree, there is nothing like spring in Duluth. Spring is intense; you feel it in your bones. Lilly's Devi didn't really get it when she tried explaining. It's unexplainable. You simply have to first experience a winter in Duluth.

"Crocuses are out. Back by the birch tree. And some of those wild violets. I think your mother planted those. I'll get our tea," Lilly says, rearranging her sari.

While Lilly is inside Sarah walks to the back of the yard and finds the violets beside the strawberry bed, and the first crocuses by the birch. She must take a walk to Chester Park to see the wild flowers. If the violets are blooming, the mayflowers should be out, and maybe the dogtooth violets and the cowslips behind St. Scholastica next to the stream near the old trap woods. Crossing the lawn to join Lilly, she notes that the yard needs a spring raking. As good as her back has been lately, she's still not up to that.

"Tom is coming to rake on Saturday," Lilly tells her, refilling their tea cups.

"He really loves his work. When he was here for dinner he talked about animals, the north woods, the lakes. He knows a great deal about Minnesota wildlife. It was the bear in Hotel Duluth that really got him into taxidermy." She tells how it was Tom's father who was the taxidermist who prepared the bear in the Black Bear Lounge of the hotel. His parents often took him along for lunch at the Black Bear, and Tom would wait for the bear to blink. He would watch out of the corner of his eye to see if it would move, perhaps moving a paw just a bit. Or if it might turn and look directly at him.

"Well, when Tom's father noticed his interest in the bear, he started teaching him about animals. And as he got older they went camping and canoeing, and then in high school Tom took an art class. He loved drawing animals and had a knack for it.

One day when he was about seventeen, his dad took him to the taxidermy shop for the first time. The first time! That surprised me. Anyway, they worked half the night on a loon and Tom became his dad's apprentice for the next 28 years. He took over the business when his father died. Quite a story," she pauses, then tells how they used to carve all the heads and bodies by hand and that's when his art really helped. Now they use Styrofoam forms.

"I saw those when I brought him the pheasant," Sarah says. They were like animal ghosts, waiting for Tom to bring them back to life. He made them seem so real. She has to admit she had a moment or two in the shop when she wondered if a snowy owl was ready to blink or turn its head. And the day she was there, the animal that seemed most like Tom was a deer. Tom is so nice and calm. And so is Lilly.

"It's strange, you being a vegetarian and he being a taxidermist, how you're friends now," Sarah says.

"True, very true," Lilly agrees.

They finish the last of their tea and Sarah gets up. "Well, I'm off to Chester Park. I need to see the spring flowers, green things. I need to think."

---

SHE TAKES THE SHORTCUT THROUGH the meadow where granite bedrock cuts through the field like a road paved with stones large as rooftops, quickly making her way along the massive flat rocks to the woods of Chester Park and the trailhead. The forest landscape is much changed since her walk with Stephen. The bright maple leaves of last fall are now filmy as lace under young green plants, and the winter snow has washed the path of leaves. She senses Stephen's presence by his absence, and for a moment it is as if a ghost walks along the path in front of her, the unseen footsteps silent on the dark compressed soil.

Last fall Stephen had seemed okay though perhaps a little melancholy and remote, but they had both laughed. Hadn't they? Yes, he had laughed when they crossed the bridge, she remembers quite clearly. Sarah stands motionless on the path. The leaves of the trees rustle overhead and the birds flutter and chirp their spring songs. Standing in a shaft of sunlight she closes her eyes to the warmth of the sun on her face.

That call from Gigi yesterday was astonishing. At first she thought it was a joke, Gigi saying Stephen was in jail, that he had stolen a religious statue from a church. It didn't make sense. But she said Stephen had been caught red-handed by a priest. He was on his way out the back door with the Madonna he had taken from an altar, a French-carved piece with gold leaf trim, considered priceless by the priest. And as if that weren't enough, a neighbor of Stephen's had seen him digging what appeared to be a grave in his backyard. The police found more religious art in the cellar of Stephen's house. Unbelievable, except it seemed to be true. Jeep was in the process of getting him out on bail.

In her disbelief, Sarah had laughed upon hearing the story, but then Gigi said quite firmly that Stephen was on the edge of sanity. Gigi confided that Stephen had spent a night with her around Christmastime, and that's when he told her of his obsessions, which he had simply considered research for his new book. But Gigi was certain he was unhinged. He talked about how beautiful it was to walk along the beach under a full moon carrying one of the statues. She said he had just spaced out describing his moon walk and didn't seem to hear her questions, and started talking to someone who wasn't in the room.

It was at this point in the phone conversation that Gigi brought up Carmen. If Gigi knew about Morgan and Carmen's relationship, which Morgan insists is over, Gigi kept it to herself. But Gigi talked about Stephen and Carmen and said that they would be a match, they're both nuts, but in a friendly and hopeful way, and that she was going to introduce them when Jeep gets Stephen out of jail.

"Oh Lord," Sarah says aloud to herself, continuing along the path and contemplating the image of Stephen sitting in a jail cell muttering to himself. And he and Carmen had already met. Seeing them across the room at the Lefse Festival was startling, so she was glad they left just shortly afterwards. "Poor Stephen."

Beneath the maple trees the forest floor is covered with mayflowers, each plant bearing a perfect white flower. The generous spacing of the plants gives an uncrowded and peaceful look to the forest floor. To Sarah, the flowers seem like a group of well-groomed seminary students. Lilly should be here to see them. Or Morgan. She and Morgan have never taken this beautiful walk together, though Chester Park is close and accessible from Lilly's house. Funny she hasn't told Lilly or Morgan about Stephen being in jail. Does everyone have a secret? It seems so lately.

She picks a lone dogtooth violet and sits beside a fallen birch. She slips a circle of birch around her wrist. The bark is smooth. The birch tree is still alive, and fresh green leaves have sprouted along its fallen branches. She stands quickly, as if discovering she had been sitting on a living creature by mistake. The tree may have bent to the ground in last week's storm, knocked down by the larger tree across its top half. Sarah starts to pull on the long slender branches, releasing the tree, branch by branch, from beneath the heavier tree trunk. After a final tug on the main branch, the young tree springs upright, its green branches swaying before settling into place. The rescued birch is slightly off center, but it looks healthy, with its roots intact, and her back seems okay, after the effort.

"MORGAN? I'M AT CHESTER PARK." This is the first time Sarah has used her new purple cell phone, and it feels strange, calling from the forest.

"Well, Hello!" Morgan says, pleased at her call. He just filled the aquarium next to the shower and was thinking of her, debating whether to release the fish into the tank before she gets home, or wait, so she can help. Two dozen white paper boxes of fish in plastic bags are lined up near the sink, looking much like Chinese takeout.

"The wildflowers are out. It's really nice here. Lots of birds too. There's a big orange mushroom down in the moss. I could take a picture of it if I knew how to work the camera."

They make a date for a walk in the woods on Saturday.

"Sarah, don't even touch the orange mushroom."

"Okay. Toadstool?"

"Right."

"All right. Bye."

Just as Sarah turns down the hill to her aunt's house, she sees the scary man from the casino pull out of the driveway in a black pickup. She cuts across the lawn and opens the door without knocking. Aunt Lilly is calmly sipping a cup of tea and sitting on a cushion in front of her Buddha. A bunch of radishes with the leaves still attached, sit at the Buddha's feet.

"Hi Lilly. Did you have a visitor?" Sarah asks, relieved to see that nothing terrible has happened." Lilly says the visitor who had just left was Hawk, and there had been some confusion but they straightened it out. It seems that Hawk is an artist, a sculptor, Lilly explains, and that the confusion was because he had her phone number, thinking it was Stephen's. It was Stephen who wanted to buy some sculpture and that's what he was calling about. Apparently it was that night you went to the casino and Morgan didn't know where you where.

Well, this Hawk was shaking like a leaf when he first came in. Said he was drinking too much coffee since he gave up chewing tobacco. He calmed down after we had a cup of tea and a nice little talk. "You know, when he first came to the door he had a smoky black aura, like a heavy shadow. It just hung there," Lilly shudders. "Then after a while, after we talked and sipped our tea, he went out to his truck and brought in a Madonna he had carved from an aged log. It was painted gold and blue but most of the paint had been scraped off. He said he liked to get an antique look and he certainly was good at that. You would have thought it was from some other time and place, even several hundred years ago. Well, I don't know if wood lasts that long. We admired the sculpture which was beautiful, very spiritual, and he became an entirely different person. He just sort of glowed. Now he's on his way to Italy. He said I may never see him again. And he said to tell Stephen to forget it, if I should see him."

"Well, that is something," Sarah says, amazed at her aunt's ability to turn such a person serene. He had quite terrified her at the casino and she hadn't even spoken with him. It was just his look. And Stephen. She'll wait to tell Lilly that Stephen is in jail. In any case, he may already be out on bail.

Morgan has changed, or is changing. Not so dramatically as Hawk, but still, in his own way. She noticed it in his tone of voice and attention to her last night when he was telling her about the mahogany from Peru and how they cut down trees that take 75 years to mature. He said the land changes, of course, and the people change. So ecologically we should use wood from our own area. Here in Minnesota we should use pine, birch, and maple. Not mahogany from Peru, which is mostly illegal anyway but you can't tell once it gets here. Then he was talking about all the different parrots they have in Peru and I could see his eyes change. He was on one subject but it seemed like he was suddenly not talking about wood or parrots but he was just looking at me. I saw a kind of infatuation in his eyes. He became quiet and we forgot about the parrots and the mahogany.

"What are the radishes for, Lilly?" Sarah asks, picking up the rosy bunch of radishes.

"A memento. They remind me of my old friend, Thor. Pastor Fjelstad. Pretty, aren't they?"

Sarah likes the bright radishes. And she likes when her aunt makes flower leis for her Buddha, now safely back in place. She forgot to look for fiddlehead ferns in the woods for Lilly. Next time. She finds the wilted dogtooth violet in her bag and sets it beside the radishes. "No fiddlehair ferns, though. I'll look on Saturday, I know you like them. I'll look on Saturday. Morgan and I are taking the Chester Creek trail. And maybe the old Stations of the Cross trail, if we get that far."

While Lilly is slicing a few radishes, Sarah decides to tell her about Stephen, and they agree it would be more likely someone like Hawk would be the one in jail, not Stephen. Lilly feels that Hawk probably spends most of his time on the dark side and she concedes that she was fortunate to get a glimpse into his brighter side. "Just like you were able to enjoy Sam Light's best side, Sarah."

"I still feel sad about Sam," she says, leaning on an elbow, suddenly tired. "It's still hard for me to believe." When Morgan told her about Sam, he gave her a copy of the police report. Sam Light, alias this and alias that, wanted in several states for fraud, forgery, theft, and possession of illegal substances.

"Sam Light wrote a book on mushrooms. Did you know that Sarah?"

"No, really?" Hearing all these things - Stephen in jail, Hawk and his sculpture, and Sam Light stealing and not at all who he was supposed to be. What's next, Lulu on Dancing with the Stars? Sarah shakes her head at the weirdness of possibilities.

"I loaned the mushroom book to Lulu," Lilly says. "I did a little investigating of my own, when Sam first arrived. And that's all I found. He fooled us all."

"Does the book have his picture?"

"Yes. It looks just like him though he's wearing glasses and he has a beard. He looks like a professor. He wrote the book with someone else but he took all the photos, and now he's in jail for twenty years," she shakes her head sadly, and raises the possibility of their visiting him sometime in jail.

"No. No I don't think so," Sarah laughs uneasily.

Lilly thinks his yoga should help Sam. Gandhi used to do yoga and meditate in jail, with all the quiet time to fill. She admires Gandhi for his convictions and how he lived so simply. They sit in silence, the only sound the crunching of their radishes, which they both dip in salt. Before Sarah leaves, they hug like as though parting for other countries.

---

SARAH DRIVES DOWN THE HILL with a lightness she hasn't felt in ages. It's springtime in Duluth, the wildflowers are blooming, she's not in jail, and she feels like singing. As soon as she passes the Amazing Grace Bakery, the whistle blows from the bridge. She is a block away by the time she stops the car, close enough to watch the bridge go up. Accustomed to the wait, she turns off the motor. Lately she finds this time waiting for a boat to go through the canal to be her best time for reflection. She is neither here nor there, and the boats and bridges have a way of inviting philosophical reflection. Just consider what a difference five minutes can make in a person's life. For instance, if she had left the taxidermy shop five minutes earlier than she did, maybe she wouldn't have been hit by the car. If Hawk had arrived at Lilly's five minutes later than he did, maybe he would have been in serious nicotine withdrawal. Might have turned mean, even strangled Lilly right in front of her Buddha and the radishes.

The bell rings and the cars begin to move. Sarah drives on, back into normal time with mundane concerns as she crosses the bridge. By the time she turns into the drive to their new house, she has the mischievous idea of sneaking in and surprising Morgan. She drives slowly and parks in the old spot, where they parked before the garage was finished. Yes, she'll surprise Morgan. Walking along the sand dune by the gardening shed, she stops. The sound of a woman's laugh comes from the house. She steps inside the shed. All of her new pots are lined up along the lower shelves, beside the potting soil and sphagnum moss. She's shaking. On the wall nearest the door is her grandfather's sand strainer. He used it to strain the sand they brought home in pails from Park Point, sifting out stones and bits of driftwood. He was a good carpenter and made the screen to last, from hard wood and with a screen just the size to cover her backyard sandbox. She runs her fingers over the screen, longing for her easy sunny childhood days.

There was only that one bad day. She was five, and started walking around the edge of the sandbox. Her mother had called her to come in for dinner but she wanted to walk all the way around the sand box, and that's when she slipped. She fell hard, her hand slamming onto the hot charcoal grill where her dad had just grilled steaks. She screamed. No one could catch her. She ran and ran, trying to out run the pain, until her mother caught her. She plunged her hand into ice water in the kitchen sink and that's when she saw the dark lines of the grill across the palm of her hand. She's holding her wrist so tight her hand is turning pale. She releases it with a gasp.

Sarah knows what she'll see if she picks up the binoculars. She hopes she's wrong. But there they are. Morgan and Carmen in the kitchen, her arms around his neck. She walks to her car like a robot and opens the door. Gets in and sits there. The dashboard looks foreign, unfamiliar. Has it always had so many gauges, so many numbers and dials? The main thing is just to get away. Drive away from here. As she starts the car she feels heat spread across her face. Her limbs feel stiff and heavy.

As she turns the corner away from the house a little boy rides past on a silver scooter. She sees him as if in a dream. He is the friendly little boy who always waves at Sarah. She waves back and her hand becomes lighter, almost weightless, and she is filled with something, a light, some glimmer of happiness in the midst of the horror, and then as soon as the boy is out of sight, the cold leaden feeling returns.

She drives mechanically. She drives past Gigi's house. Doesn't want to see Gigi. Doesn't want to see Jeep. Doesn't want to hear about Stephen. She doesn't want to see Lilly. Pity and understanding she doesn't need. What she needs is a gun. She could drive straight up to Target. She could drive up to Leif's at the Chester Park caretaker's house. She could hire Leif to kill Carmen. Or Morgan. Or both of them. Or, she could do it herself and then she could go to jail with Sam and Stephen.

She slows down on Sixth Avenue and pulls into the alley beside Tom Troll's Taxidermy shop. She wipes away a tear, and begins to clean the dashboard with the teary tissue. Maybe Hawk is at the airport waiting for his flight to Italy. She could go there too; advertise her class in yoga in an historic setting.

Tom Troll is putting away his tools for the day when he spots Sarah sitting in her car. He watches from the door of his shop as she cleans the inside of the car with a tissue. She cries and then laughs. Now she's scrubbing the inside front window. What should he do? He wants to help but then he doesn't want to interfere either. He looks around the shop for just the right animal, then remembering that she likes fish, decides on a large-mouthed bass. He walks slowly toward Sarah's car, his steps so hesitant that he might be walking backwards if he weren't walking forwards. He takes off his hat and holds the fish up to the front windshield. If he smiles kindly, perhaps that will help Sarah. He smiles his most polite smile.

"Sarah," he says.

"Tom." She opens the window and sits back against the car seat.

"I have some fish chowder that's still warm in the shop. I just put it in the refrigerator. Would you like some?"

Startled, she thanks him, but says no thanks. She knows he saw her acting crazy and half hysterical and she appreciates his silence on the subject. "I was thinking of going to the Black Bear Casino. Do you want to go?" she asks Tom.

———————

THEY SIT SIDE-BY-SIDE at the Go Fish machines, each with a cup of Coke next to their respective plastic bucket of nickels. Sarah is playing like she hasn't a care in the world, here in the casino where the real world slips so easily away. Tom laughs loudly at his fisherman's catch. She has never heard Tom laugh before. If it weren't for all the smoke, she'd like to live here. Just playing the games, drinking Coke. She likes the abandonment of reality and the decadence of gambling. She also likes that she can go look at the fish by the back entrance whenever she likes. The hell with reality.

She hasn't seen the Moon Madness guy yet. Maybe tonight it will be someone different. Maybe a big chicken, or someone in a seagull costume. Tom would like that. She chuckles to herself. Who cares about Carmen anyway. Probably she just stopped by. Maybe they were saying goodbye. Maybe she is going to see Stephen in jail. What could Stephen and Carmen possibly have in common? That tall fisherman in the game looks a little like Morgan. Quarters come pouring out of the machine. It's a good day for Go Fish. She likes the sound of the money crashing down into the metal tray. Tom's nickels are silent. He catches his nickels in his hand before they can touch the metal bin. He doesn't miss a nickel. She likes these old machines better than the new ones that give you paper tickets instead of coins.

"Hey, Sarah," Jessie taps Sarah's machine in greeting and laughs. "Having fun?" "Oooh, look at you with all those quarters! So are you going to let me do your hair, do you think? Green? Oh, hi Tom. You're winning too, hey?"

Sarah wants her hair green. Spring green, she tells Jessie, without hesitation. Yes, she wants to live in the casino and have green hair. "Are you still doing hair at the hospital?"

"Every Thursday. Oh there's Rolf. I'd better go. Call me now and we'll set a date. Don't forget! See you," she rushes off.

Sarah and Tom dump their coins into the change machine. They are both surprised at how much they receive for their buckets of coins. They decide to take a break from gambling and find themselves a table in the Lady Slipper Lounge, which is deserted except for a guy in a plaid shirt hunched over a beer at the bar.

They're both excited and exhausted. At their little table Sarah takes the small paperback book of Frost poems from her purse and skims the index for a poem that might be relevant. Nothing pops up and she's blurry eyed. Tonight she'll look again in bed, except now she doesn't have a bed if she's going to live in the casino. "Oh, this," she says. "On a Tree Fallen across the Road." She tells Tom that's her life now. Tom surprises her by how knowledgeable he is about Robert Frost, more so than she is. Tom excuses himself.

While he's gone, she reads the poem again, thinking of all the trees that have fallen across her roads. That Carmen. What kind of a name is that anyway. She looks more like a Freida or Katarina.

There's Jessie. Maybe she could do her hair tonight. She hurries across the aisle to catch up. Jessie is with Rolf beside the fish tank. Says she wants it green, tonight if possible. Jessie

advealpalall

laughs and says, why not? We're just on our way out and you might as well come along.

Sarah sees Tom leaving the phone both and calls to him and gestures that she's going with Jessie so she doesn't need a ride. She waves and leaves with Jessie and Rolf.

"But Sarah," Tom says, mostly to himself. They've disappeared into the dark of the parking lot by the time he steps through the door. He should have shouted. He should have caught up with her, told her. But how? He knows there was some terrible misunderstanding. Whenever Carmen is in the picture it seems there is some kind of trouble, but Carmen had stopped by to say goodbye to Morgan and to tell him about the tower. She knew someone on the University of Wisconsin's Board of Trustees who knew someone who had just heard that Morgan's tower project had been approved for construction. She had come to tell him the good news and was so happy. And now Sarah has disappeared again and Morgan was making himself sick with worry. Tom should have called right away, not played Go Fish all that time. And now Sarah's gone off and he doesn't know where to find Jessie or Rolf. He stands beside the fish tank of loneliness considering the evening's dilemma when he sees a giant corn cob walk down the aisle past the black jack tables. The corn cob stops beside Tom.

"Got a match?" he asks Tom, who has none. "Ah, never mind. My corn silk might catch. Damn itchiest outfit. You mind watching my sign a minute?"

The corn cob heads for the men's room before he can answer. Tom waits patiently beside the fish tank and the sign which reads.

MR CORN ON THE CASH
Midnight Give-away – 1 a.m.

# *two*

---

STEPHEN HASN'T HAD THIS much attention from women in years. Just what is so appealing about a man in prison, anyway? Gigi said it's the fallen angel image they like, but Stephen knows he's no angel, fallen or otherwise. He doesn't even know why he stole the Madonna from the church, except it was there. He had only come to sit in a peaceful place and then once he started looking at her eyes he saw how she was calling to him and that's the last he remembers, before he got caught. He does remember sweat running into his eyes though, and some primitive excitement like he wasn't even human. He doesn't know why he didn't accept bail. He could have, but in some way he knew he had to be incarcerated. It felt right.

Carmen has sent him a box of Godiva chocolates every week he's been in jail until this past week when she delivered them herself. It was good, being with Carmen in Duluth. She's beautiful. She's smart. He knows she's the same person now, but he was so glad when she left today. He's really been surprised that it's his neighbor from the writer's group, Laura, whom he has come to depend on. Each week she writes him an actual letter, sometimes including a poem, a funny little poem that cheers him up, gives him hope. He told his counselor that he might be falling in love with her, and at first that was a half lie, but now it's true, or almost true.

He can't fathom his lawyer. He's abrupt and sure of himself. What can Stephen do? A person has to trust his

174

lawyer, go along more or less blindly. If what he says is true, he can be out after the hearing, do his community service and his church work. He can put it all behind him and get back to his book. Thank heavens he's on sabbatical this year. It gives him some time, hopefully, to be forgiven. And he is grateful for all the good advice he's getting, and for the confidence everyone seems to have in him. He sure doesn't have it himself. How can he be sure he won't do it again? He can't. He'll have to take it one day at a time. Join some twelve step program for thieves.

Dr. Bellini wants him to keep a journal. He calls it a journal of introspection. The challenge is to be the detective of his own soul, and write anything that comes to mind about himself and how he ended up in this predicament. And he is to think about what he could do to be a more mentally stable person. This morning his entry was short: "I don't like to be alone," he wrote. It took him most of the morning to come up with that. Since lunch he's been hearing Greta Garbo say, "I want to be alone." She says it even slower than in the movie. "I want to be alone," he repeats under his breath, He has yet to tell Dr. Bellini about the voices, though he doesn't hear James Cagney every day now. Maybe every other day. Stephen opens his journal and edits his entry, changing "I don't like to be alone" to "I don't want to be alone."

"Better" the Greta voice says. "More poetic."

Yes, much better," he agrees, then looks around to see if the guard is nearby. He doesn't' want any reports that he's talking to himself. At least he only hears one voice at a time, though it wouldn't surprise him to hear them both. He wouldn't want them to discuss him, leaving him out of the conversation entirely like he didn't even exist. But they wouldn't do that. They seem to care about him, at least so far.

"Maybe I'm like Saint Francis," he writes in his journal. "The angels look after me." He pauses. Is that okay? If Dr.

Bellini reads that, would he end up asking about the voices? Would Stephen forget and just start talking about Marlene Dietrich or Greta Garbo or James Cagney? Stephen decides to leave the entry. Yes, and mentioning the angels makes him seem spiritual and possibly on the right path. Which may be true. Might be. It's hard to tell what Bellini would think. Isn't that a sandwich, a bellini? He can't remember. Seems when he used to visit his old roommate in Brooklyn they used to get something called a bellini at the deli. Or panini? Or were those the blintzes? He shakes his head. Everything used to be clear. Everything used to be easy. When Jeannie was alive.

Stephen lies back on his bumpy cot and looks at the card he received from Sarah. It's a photograph of a black wolf with penetrating eyes. Her note says that she has been reading Robert Frost and that she's sorry he's in jail. He's read her note several times, looking for some hidden meaning or special message but he gets nothing more than a possible reference to their walk at Chester Park in the fall where they spoke about Frost and his birch trees. He pictures her face that day when he pretended to lock her inside the tennis court and they looked at each other through the fence with the crimson ivy. He never understood Sarah, but he suspects she's more like him than anyone else he's known. She might steal a Madonna. Gigi never would, nor Carmen. Nor Laura, though she would understand someone might want to do that. Sarah has a mad streak, definitely. It's in the eyes of the wolf. But why hadn't she written more? Did she think they read his mail? Do they? Oh, she was probably just sending a thoughtful note.

His lawyer says he's lucky the local jail was full and he was placed here in the juvenile detention center in his own room. He knows that's true, but still he hates hearing the crying at night. If he can fall asleep soon after lights out, he's okay. But if he can't get to sleep or wakes in the night he hears the crying, a soft hopeless crying which goes on and on and makes him think of crickets, because it's always the same, endless and repetitious, he'll have a bad night. Last night Marlene Dietrich talked to him until he could go back to sleep. "It's just the sorrow of the world. That's why they cry," she had said.

Stephen drops the wolf card and falls asleep. When he wakes, it is the middle of the night and his pillow is soaked with his own tears and he hears the sad crying down the corridor and footsteps of a guard walking away. But staring into the darkness he feels hope, like some hurdle has been crossed.

———

STEPHEN CAN HARDLY TAKE his eyes off the oak table in front of him. The grain of wood is interesting with its curving patterns which turn into oval eyes and even mouths. There is a landscape with mountains coming out from the other side of his lawyer's notebook. Oh he knows he's lucky. It usually takes much longer before you get your hearing. Between the cancellation of one case, and Jeep's help, he knows that's how he got here this soon. Now someone has set a bottle Perrier in front of him. And a straw. Well that's odd.

His one male friend, Andrew, is sitting in the front row with all of Stephen's women friends. He came all the way from the Iron Range to be here, even though he didn't even have to come. None of them had to come. They've all been interviewed and recorded and transcribed and videotaped. Kiwanis club Fred is sitting in the back row by himself. He'll probably put something about the hearing in his monthly minutes to read at the writer's club. That will be something to deal with, if he really gets to go home again, seeing Fred every day out mowing his lawn and all. Probably he would act nice and friendly and then sneak in little spy-type questions when they're out raking their lawns.

Sarah and Lilly are sitting together. He doesn't see Morgan. Stephen heard Lilly's singing bowl when he first came in and that helped calm him down. Carmen is sitting on the other side of Lilly, and then Gigi, and Laura is on the end. There are three priests in the row behind the women, and then some social services people. His psychologist is sitting by himself on the other side with a notebook. There's Morgan, walking down the aisle. He sits in the row with Stephen's psychologist. He had forgotten what a striking impression Morgan makes, like a movie star or famous person, except that he looks like he forgot something. Maybe it's that he didn't finish combing his hair. He shouldn't stare. Stephen doesn't know why he's looking at everyone like he can see them but they can't see him. He's not registering things right. Better just to look at the table and sip his Perrier.

He must stay in control. That's absolutely necessary. What really worries him is they might bring in the Madonna he stole, or one of the ones he bought from Hawk. But his lawyer said this wasn't a trial and they wouldn't bring physical evidence like that. Still, he already feels sweat on his face just thinking what he would do if they did. You never know what twists can occur, like in a Perry Mason trial. What if there is someone really clever like Jessica Fletcher from "Murder She Wrote?" But he didn't murder anyone. It just feels like he did. The whole atmosphere in this room is unnerving, full of past ghosts probably. He's starting to feel like he's floating, or in some dream sleep. What if people start walking past his table each holding a Madonna and he will be asked to identify each one. They might hold them out right into his face so he can smell the wood, the mold. Last night he had a bad dream about Hawk. It pops into his memory with a jolt. Now anything can happen in a situation like this.

"Take it easy," James Cagney says. "It's no big deal. Just relax, you'll be fine."

They've started. He's blanking it out. Stephen sees their mouths move but he can't hear. It's like a TV with no sound. What's happening? But he doesn't have to say anything. That's what his lawyer said. All he has to do is sit there.

"Just drink your juice," Cagney says. "Relax Stephen."

Stephen repeats the words to himself: *Relax Stephen, drink your juice.* Probably they didn't even have Perrier in Cagney's time. Just booze. Pretend it's a gin and tonic.

His lawyer talks for a long time. Or is it a short time? He can't tell. He repeats his mantra, *Relax Stephen, drink your juice.* He has the feeling that Lilly is right beside him holding his hand and when he closes his eyes he sees a stuffed seagull, which doesn't bother him. Quite the contrary. He really does feel relaxed and he still can't hear the voices. His psychologist is speaking now, forming words with his lips that Stephen can't hear. He's blanked it all out. Someone, something is helping him.

"Shhh," he hears Marlene Dietrich whisper in his ear. "It is finished. It's all over."

A man comes to his table and offers his hand. The first regular words he can hear are "Congratulations, Stephen Spine." The priests shake his hand, one after the other. Gigi kisses his cheek. Everyone is around him and Laura smiles so kindly that he knows it's going to be all right. They must have declared him all right to go home. He can do his penance for the community and the church, visit a probation officer for a time, and a counselor. He wants to do the church work, he really does. Life will get back to normal. It's going to be all right. It's going to be good. How strange is justice.

---

ON THE PLANE SARAH HAS the window seat. She leans her cheek against the window and looks at the stars, each star as beautiful and mysterious as the people she knows. She can see

Mars, reddish and bright, like Morgan. He is beside her working on an equation that covers several pages of his notebook. He keeps flipping back and forth between pages, adding more detail until the pages are dense with figures. It has to do with a filter system for telescopes that selectively eliminate light close to the earth, the light pollution from cities. Next month she is going with him to a science convention in Zurich where he will present his paper. She is excited about seeing the Alps, riding the trains, going to museums and beautiful churches. She has a book on Paul Klee from the library and knows Zurich has some of his major works.

Will Morgan and Carmen cross paths again in the future? She doesn't know, but tonight it doesn't seem to matter. Carmen seemed ecstatic about her new job in Washington, D.C. at the Smithsonian. Sarah hopes she will be so busy with her work, her committees, and social events, that she will be completely satisfied and much too busy to pursue Morgan. Carmen is sure to find someone else.

Even Stephen should be okay. He looked bewildered after the hearing, but happy too. She met his psychologist who seemed cheerful and bright. Stephen introduced him as Dr. Pannini, but the psychologist referred to himself as Bill. Bill Bellini. What a weird hearing it was with Stephen humming through most of it. What was he thinking? But his lawyer made him out to be an angel, a true spiritual person.

She's sleepy, looking out at the stars. Which one is Stephen? Is he a shooting star, to be seen only by chance? Or are they all like that? Or perhaps they are both shooting stars and more solid and predictable as well, like the Milky Way. In Duluth she loves to stand outside and wonder at the Milky Way as it flows down across the sky like a thick beautiful bridge of stars. She refused to listen when Morgan said the Milky Way was really quite transient, considering eternity. Is that a word scientists use? Sarah doesn't like to hear anything scientific about the stars or the universe being transient. She only wants the mystery and beauty of a moment.

Although it is late and most of the passengers have turned out their lights and are resting during the short flight to Duluth, the Captain's voice comes over the speaker system. He says if you are seated on the right side of the plane you'll be able to see the Northern Lights putting on a nice little show.

Sarah and Morgan are on the left side. Earlier Lilly had moved from her aisle seat by Morgan to an empty seat by the window on the right. Lilly beckons to Sarah to take the empty seat beside her and points to another empty seat in the row in front for Morgan but he smiles and keeps at his calculations. Sarah joins Lilly, and they lean shoulder to shoulder, watching the greenish white lights flicker and curl upward in waves dancing across the sky. Lilly tells of a Native American legend of the aurora borealis being the spirits of the past who come to visit, bringing hope to those still on the earth.

Morgan squeezes into the seat with Sarah. They all lean toward the lights, which pulsate like some great heart monitor of the heavens, like the very breath of the universe. Morgan slips his hand under Sarah's shirt and runs his fingers up and down her back. She wants to stay in the airplane forever watching the Northern Lights while Morgan runs his fingers up and down her spine. She wonders just how happy a person can be without going mad.

---

BACK IN DULUTH, Sarah finds messages on the answering machine. One is from the library: the lost Ginsberg book has been found so she can stop looking for that. The other message is from Kathy Wilson, about the house at Grand Marais. Yes, if Sarah still wants to use the house for a retreat next week please call to let her know.

Morgan has a call from UMD, one from a construction guy, and one from Carmen. Carmen's message is addressed to them both:

"Hi Sarah. Hi Morgan." Sarah's name first, like Sarah was Carmen's best friend. Ha Ha. She is mailing them a book on shore birds that she found on the internet.

Morgan wants to know about the retreat and if Sarah really wants to do that. He looks skeptical and curious at the same time. Kathy Wilson is Lulu's cousin in Apple Valley. Sarah and Lilly and Lulu were talking one day over tea, about taking a week off to be alone, somewhere not in your own house, someplace where you didn't know anyone, to just experience – oh, how did Lilly put it? Just to see how you do, see how you change. Lilly had encouraged Sarah when Lulu mentioned Kathy and their vacation house up near the Canadian border on the shore of Lake Superior. Lilly thought a retreat would help Sarah, that it would be more helpful than the Black Bear Casino.

In a way Sarah wants to do the retreat for herself, but also to see what Morgan would do while she is gone. Can she be more balanced, more appreciative of life? She wants to find out.

She decides to call Kathy in the morning and tell her she would like to stay at the house up north next week. Lulu said that's how they refer to it – "the house up north." She needs this retreat and tells Morgan that it would be her version of his living in a jungle laboratory in a tree. Lulu had reminded her that there was another connection she had to the house. Sarah's parents were friends with the people who lived there before Kathy and Lowell. She does recall their talking about a house up north near Grand Marais but she hadn't realized until recently that it was the same house she would be visiting. She's excited! But Sarah doesn't tell Morgan how she also recalls hearing about the wolves howling at night from the nearby forest.

"Yes, I'm definitely going next week," she tells Morgan. "I see," he says, climbing into bed, unsure if she's well and stable enough for the trip yet hopeful that she may find some strength and happiness to take back with her, some peace of mind.

Sarah climbs into bed. She looks at Morgan looking at her and sees kindness in his dark eyes, and a hint of timber wolf.

# three

SARAH DRIVES AS FAR as Two Harbors and Morgan drives the rest of the way to Grand Marais. Kathy's directions are excellent and they find the short cut to the old highway outside of Grand Marais easily. Finding the house is more difficult and Sarah worries they will be late. Morgan is unconcerned and slows down to read the numbers on a mail box, just beyond a meadow of Black Angus cattle. They're getting close. Sarah tries to relax. Kathy and Lowell are going to stay at the house long enough to show them around before their drive back to Apple Valley. After a few more hills they come to the Wilson's mailbox and turn up the steep road toward the house.

Kathy and Lowell are happy to see them and seem not to notice that they are late. The view of the lake from the house is spectacular and Sarah is delighted at the prospect of the week ahead. Lowell walks them through the house, explaining the fireplace, the phone system, the complicated upstairs radio, and all the thermostats. In the basement Kathy points out the peculiarities of the washer and dryer and shows Sarah where to find the bird seed. While Lowell is showing them the Audubon field guilds and the binoculars in the den, they hear a noise, quite a substantial thud. They all turn toward the sound. Lowell says it's a bird, and they follow him outside to the front of the house where the sound came from.

It was a partridge, all fluffed up and dead in the grass, the color of fall leaves. There was a wet smear on the window where it crashed, no doubt confused by the glare of the bright fall sun. Lowell picked it up and its head hung loose like a sock full of wet berries, and Sarah knew from her partridge hunting days how warm its body must feel. She sighed, not just for its death, but as a vegetarian lament, for the one item most difficult to give up, and the remembrance of a plate of tender partridge stew, complete with onions, potatoes and carrots, wafted through the fall air of her imagination, hanging there with Lowell's question: Do you want it? She was not proud of how long it took her to say no. She watched him walk off with the partridge and toss it into the ravine on the far side of the apple trees.

"Well," he said when he got back to the house.

They stood looking at the apple trees closest to the house, and Sarah was thinking about bears as she looked at the shapes in the spaces between the dark low branches. She had the feeling Lowell was thinking about bears too.

Lowell said the bears had gone off to find dens, after pretty much cleaning out the apples. There were a few Firesides left in the trees, big green apples at the feathery ends of the higher branches, and a few still on the ground, but the crab apple trees in the ravine were still dotted with clusters of small red apples.

Morgan and Sarah walked Kathy and Lowell to their car. They had a five-hour drive to Minneapolis ahead, and wanted to beat the rush hour traffic. Morgan wanted to spend the first night with Sarah but she insisted that if it was going to be a real retreat she had to start it off by herself. She promised to call if she had problems but made Morgan promise not to call her except in an emergency. She watched with some trepidation as he drove away toward Duluth.

As soon as Morgan was out of sight it was noticeable how isolated she was there in northern Minnesota; alone for a week, surrounded by dense forests and the open expanse of Lake Superior. Even the sky seemed different – bigger, and more conspicuous than in the city. She found herself listening to the quiet like it was a particular note that held everything together and she just hadn't noticed before, or not for a long time. The quiet was everywhere: in the lake and the sky and underneath the ground and there was a heavy quiet in the trees, and she found herself breathing deeply of the piney air.

Sarah took a chair on the porch that faced the lake. She sat on the porch with her feet propped on a sun-bleached moose antler. Although she and Morgan had lived on Park Point for several months now, she had never just sat like this. With a new house there was always something to do. Or was it that she just hadn't taken the time to relax. Here by herself she couldn't get enough of the sparkling blue lake and all the shades of blue dissolving into one another under the lazy afternoon clouds. She took in the blue of the lake like a transfusion of blood, and it wasn't long before she started to feel stronger and somehow more herself, or like she was draining back into herself, her long lost self. It was well into the afternoon when she left the porch.

The house was spacious and had a nice fireplace. She walked through the house to familiarize herself with the various rooms and to review the location of the three thermostats. She took an unreasonably long time to decide whether to use the bear towels, or the moose towels, and her hands were dry by the time she decided on the bears. She admired the birch logs by the fireplace, and the baskets of birch bark and wondered if they were actually to burn, or just to look at. The book shelves had plenty of books on trolls, wildlife, hiking trails, rocks, trees, beaches, agates, fishing, canoeing, waterfalls, and Scandinavian humor. She opens a humor book to a random page. Why do Norwegians use only salt and pepper? Because using a fancy herb or spice would draw attention to itself, and would be considered "showing off" by the cook.

---

186

BY THE TIME SHE WAS comfortable with the house there was perhaps an hour or so of daylight left. Still, she was anxious to get into the woods while she could. She laced her hiking boots and headed for the woods, following the open area along the telephone line behind the house. Because the ground was dry, the sound of crisp rustling leaves and her boots breaking small twigs seemed considerably amplified as she walked along a deer trail that cut through birch, pine and dogwood. She stopped at the base of an elegant old birch tree to admire the platform of a deer blind built in the crook of its high thick branches.

It was easy climbing the boards that made up the ladder nailed to the tree, and with her fresh blue blood she easily climbed up from the branches onto the firm wooden platform. It was wonderful to be up in a tree as an adult, and so far from civilization. She felt like something wild that lived in a tree. Sarah could see past the house to a wide golden meadow edged with birch groves, and the dark blue lake beyond. The air smelled sweet, like a stew of berries, fresh leaves and spongy moss. She could hear the quiet sound of water in a nearby brook, and follows its meandering path toward the lake. The sharp cry of a crow brought her out of her reverie, and she was ready to climb back down, at least for today.

But the tree seemed to have risen. However did she get up so high, and with her back? And what if she broke a leg? No one would find her for a week, not until Saturday, when Morgan was coming up. She tossed her hat down, and then her scarf, and contemplated how best to turn around so she could take a giant step to the crook of the birch from where she could reach the ladder. This was a considerable decision, because she could see no way to turn around without crisscrossing her legs in a highly unnatural manner. And there seemed no logical handhold within reach. She took a firm grip on the nearest limb with one hand, twisted against the tree, and dangled herself slowly downward, like an old monkey, until her foot reached the crook of the birch, and from there it was simply a matter of climbing down the ladder to the safety of the ground.

Back on firm ground, Sarah was unsteady and shaken. She picked up her hat and scarf, and was surprised to see she had torn a hole in the knee of her pants, but the small rip put her in a gleeful mood. "Just like a kid," she said to herself. The sun was beginning to set by the time she reached the back door, and her back felt fine.

———

AFTER DINNER SHE MADE an excellent birch log fire, and went to bed much earlier than she would have in the city, falling asleep almost as soon as her head settled onto the pillow with the purple bears walking around its edges.

Late that night she awoke to a fluttering sound. It came from the curtains. She sat bolt upright, yet remained calm. It was very dark, as she had turned off the night light before she climbed into bed. The shadow of something appeared at the top edge of the open curtains, somewhat like the shadow of a large bird, a curved, fluffy shape, apparently formed by moonlight on the lampshade, or perhaps the spindle at the side of the dresser mirror, and she was very drowsy and comfortable as she contemplated the shape.

"It's good to see you. I'm glad you didn't make me into a stew."

Her father's voice. Sarah got up and turned on the light. She pulled the cord to close the drapes, then opened them again. There was no shadow and she didn't know where to look. In her disorientation, she looked out the window at the stars.

"Dad?"

No answer. She just stood there in the middle of the room, for how long she couldn't say. Her father had been dead for nine years. Sarah put on her red slippers and went downstairs.

She wasn't nervous as she waited for the cocoa to heat, but she knew she wasn't in any normal state either. Better not to think, except about the cocoa, how smooth and warm it was going to be. As she stirred the cocoa, he spoke again.

"I'm here."

She didn't startle. She pretended not to be surprised. And somehow she wasn't especially. It was so late, and so far north, at the edge of everything – the rim of the great lake Gitche Gumee and hundreds of miles of dense forest filled with timber wolves and black-eyed moose, forests spreading north and spilling across the great Canadian border. Anything seemed possible. And of course her mom and dad used to stay here, before the Johnsons willed the house to Kathy and Lowell. Lulu hadn't known that, though Lilly may have known. Sarah remembered hearing about how they made wine in the basement and the equipment and bottles were still down there; she saw them when Kathy was explaining the eccentricities of the washer and dryer. And Lowell pointed out how her dad had painted some of the woodwork in the house. Earlier she had touched the paint, felt the brushstrokes of that odd orangey color in the downstairs bathroom when she was trying to decide about the towels. It seemed almost natural and normal – part of the dimension of being so far north, and her automatic response was just to go along, to bide her time.

"The partridge?" she said taking a sip of cocoa.

"Yes," he said, and Sarah thought he sounded sad.

"Why did you fly into the window then?"

"To get your attention. I had to be dramatic."

She started up the steep stairs with her cocoa, holding the warm moose mug like it was the holy grail. She had to concentrate hard to keep her hands from trembling as she climbed the stairs. She turned out the light and settled herself in the bedroom chair, holding the warm ceramic mug with both hands for solace and support. She sipped and waited and contemplated the possibility that her deceased dad had come to visit in the form of a partridge, a dead partridge's shadow.

"Did it hurt?" she asked, to see if he was in the room.

There was quite a pause before he answered, and she was starting to think it was gone, or that she was just waking up.

"No," he said then in a solemn manner. "I'm just a spirit now you know, but I was sad for the bird. It was hard. I had to drink a couple of beers before I did it, and still my spiritual advisors had to throw me up into the air. I closed my eyes when I hit."

"Well," Sarah said, thinking she would probably close her eyes too. "It hurts," she says, touching her chest in confusion. "Why did you come?"

"I don't know, except that I had to, just once more. I started thinking about fudge, how good it was."

"You made really good fudge, " Sarah said. "Really smooth."

The drapes rustled behind her.

"Good bye," she heard in a now-muffled voice.

"Wait!" Sarah got up, and reached high into the drapes, but he was gone and she let go of the empty material.

She stood looking out the window toward where Lowell said the Northern Lights appear, which is of course north though she would have looked toward the lake if he hadn't told her. A low white light swept across the sky, and ghostly shapes swirled upward in a crazy dance of light. But there were no colors like on the plane, only white.

The Northern Lights? Or was this just a beacon with a low and rhythmic light coming from Grand Marais. She watched the crazy swirls of light and dancing shapes not knowing what she was seeing; there was no pilot to tell her what was happening.

It had been a long day, riding all the way up to Grand Marais and climbing the tree and all. She decided to turn out the light, climb back into bed with her cocoa, and think about fudge. All those dark winter nights when it was too cold to skate, the bright kitchen felt extra cozy, especially when they made fudge. She liked helping, and she liked the rules. It made life seem orderly and controllable. Butter the pan so the sugar doesn't crystallize. Use the wooden spoon. Boil to the soft ball state. Test by letting the fudge drip off the spoon into a jelly glass of cold water. Let it sink to the bottom of the glass until it forms a syrupy chocolate blob. Run cold water in the sink. Stir fudge over cold water, add butter, and keep stirring until it shines. Leave the pan in cold water until the fudge begins to set, then spread on waxed paper before it gets too hard to spread.

The kitchen was crowded when everyone came to check on the fudge: her mom and brothers and her grandfather, but her dad was in charge and she was his chief helper. They made the fudge together. Her mom poured milk and made tea, and Sarah settled down at the kitchen table beside her grandfather with a glass of milk and a large piece of perfect creamy chocolate fudge.

Sarah slurps the last of her cocoa and the old fudge ceremony slips away, but she retains the peacefulness in her sleepiness. Ready to drift off, she tries to keep a small space open so she can hear the voice again, if it returns. She watches the lights in the sky from the bed, but hears nothing further, nor are there any more bird-like shadows in the drapes. Finally she can no longer keep her eyes open and she falls asleep.

The next morning Sarah is refreshed and energetic and puts aside thoughts of the night before as one would put aside a half-remembered dream. She attributes the peculiar events to be a consequence of a first night alone in this large house on Lake Superior, nothing more. She did her morning routine of yoga exercises and a ten-minute meditation, then took her breakfast of coffee and toast with honey out to the porch to enjoy the morning sun. She was feeling at home, and perused the Cook County News that Lowell and Kathy had left behind, noting the Musher's Clinic planned for next month. That she would have to miss, not that she knows anything about dog sled racing, but it sounds intriguing. But this Tuesday night there is something: Sawtooth Mountain Clinic Foot Care – Senior Center. Please bring your own bucket, towel and soap. She wiggles her toes at this possibility, but concludes it is probably just for seniors. Then on page five there is a photograph of three dead ruffed grouse, "harvested this week." Too sad. But she likes the color photo on the front page of autumn trees along the Gunflint Trail.

———

AFTER BREAKFAST SHE TAKES the same path as before but this time continues through the meadow until it comes out onto a dirt road. She follows the road to a clearing where an empty pickup is parked beside several neat stacks of birch logs and a chain saw is buzzing somewhere in the woods. Continuing down the road she soon comes to a hand-made sign that reads "The Holy Land." She finds it easy to agree with that, especially on such a crisp sunny day with all the leaves shining in the sun. She turns around at this point and by the time she gets back to the clearing of stacked logs, a man in a red hat is sawing. His hat stands out like a bright red bird against the white birch logs, and Sarah is a bit self conscious because she too is wearing a red hat. The sawing is the only sound for miles, and its low monotonous hum seems like a chant. Perhaps she was staring, because he stops sawing and turns toward Sarah.

"Hi, I'm Jacque. Good day for cutting wood. Do you like birch?"

"I do. I like the birch bark," she tells him, and feels like he knows she climbed the tree yesterday and almost got stuck, the way he looks at her. His eyes are like no blue eyes she has ever seen. He skin is dark, and his face is angular and almost regal, and from the way he stands she can tell he's at home in the woods. His ponytail hangs down his back like a shiny mane, and spirals of wavy curls form a Botticelli-like halo above his eyes. Sarah steps backwards.

"French, Cree and Finnish," he says, in answer to her unasked question.

"Oh," she replies. "I'm Sarah, the Norwegian." Her reply makes them both laugh and she sees his white teeth.

"I'd better get back," she says and starts down the road, surprised that her feet feel large and ungainly, as if she's wearing some modified version of clown shoes instead of normal hiking boots.

"Sarah, wait. Would you like to make a coffin?"

"No, I don't think so," she says, speeding up, thinking either he's crazy or he has a really peculiar sense of humor.

"Seven o'clock, tonight at the high school," he calls out. She can sense him watching her climb the hill , and is glad to reach the turnoff to the house. But here is another sign, an old wooden sign that no longer has a message, but probably once said No Hunting. She ponders what one might put on such a blank sign as she heads through the high grass of the clearing. What message would be appropriate, would measure up to the ingenuity of The Holy Land? A Smoky the Bear fire prevention sign? Then again, No Hunting would do, she decides. The ghost letters of the old sign could be traced and repainted.

The short fall day passes quickly, and by dusk she has replenished the birch bark in the baskets, and set fresh birch logs beside the fireplace. She turns the piano light on low and leaves the other lights off in order to enjoy the transition from day to night. After lighting the fire, she guiltily helps herself to one of Lowell's fancy ales from the refrigerator. She fluffs the wild rice on the stove. It's just right: tender, but still crunchy, and nice and buttery.

It's dark by the time she finishes her supper and spots the deer out by the clothes line. She can see them well with just the one light on in the house, four white-tailed deer, skittish, but still taking their time to sniff about. They move past the garage, a young buck and three does, flicking their white tails as they move down toward the mailbox. The buck crosses the road before the light of a car nears the group, but the three smaller deer run back up into the yard. She uses the binoculars to watch the buck in the meadow. He stands still as a statue waiting for the others, but they were too frightened, and eventually he crosses back into the yard and they all run into the upper woods behind the house.

That night Sarah has a normal night's sleep, and the next two nights as well. The following day she drives Lowell's old truck into town and after drooping off a film, she stops at the Howlin' Wolf, curious to see what the place looks like after reading about it in the paper, but it's closed. She drives down to the lake and parks, planning to pick up a few donuts from the World's Best Donut shop, but a Closed for the Season sign hangs on the front door. A man comes up behind Sarah and sighs loudly. She asks about the Screaming Trout and he says it was the Angry Trout and it was closed too. They watch a pine cone drop to the sidewalk. She has never in her life actually seen a pine cone drop right out of a tree.

"Tree turd," the man says, then walks away mumbling about what kind of town is it where everything is closed and you can't even get a donut. She picks up the pine cone and drives over to the conveniently open convenience store, and buys a paper, one of the local blue recycling bags, and some ale to replenish Lowell's refrigerator stock.

---

BACK HOME TO ANOTHER NIGHT and still no talking partridge. She is nearly asleep, watching a bright twinkling star and trying to recall its name, when she hears a tinkling sound and then a rustling in the drapes.

"Dad?" she asks in a childish voice.

"Yes, it is I."

"My. You didn't used to talk like that. So formal."

"We all change."

"Well. I thought you were really gone again."

"I forgot something."

"Yes?"

"I've watched you for some time now, sitting on the floor early in the morning, cross-legged like a child in Kindergarten, with your hands on your knees and your eyes closed. When you first sit down you hum like a fog horn. Why do you do that? That's what I've been wondering. Are you calling a boat? Do you want to travel?"

"Fog horn? Oh, the Om sound. It is like a fog horn, isn't it? I just hadn't noticed before. That's the universal hum of the universe. I would have thought you'd know that, being dead all these years, in the spirit world and all."

"Oh, we don't know everything. That's real interesting about the universal hum because that's pretty much where I live, or exist, rather. Well, I have to get back now. I won the bet, since you said it is like a fog horn, even though it isn't, exactly."

"You live in the universal hum?"

"Well, it's more like . . . remember when we played the comb covered with a piece of waxed paper?"

"Yes, sure. It felt funny. It buzzed - made your lips vibrate."

"That's what it's like. Only you don't have the lips."

"My."

"I'd better go now. Good bye."

"Wait!"

"Yes?"

"Thanks for all the good fudge."

"You're welcome."

"Will you come again?"

But he was gone, and somehow even without an answer, Sarah knew he wouldn't be back. She could hardly believe it, but she really saw a shooting star right then out the window. And she felt good too, not at all sad or confused.

———————

THE NEXT NIGHT SHE FOUND the shop class at the high school by following a man carrying a long plank.

"Hey, Sarah, glad to see you," Jacque says when she enters the room. There are four men and two women, already busy working on their coffins, and Jacque introduces everyone.

"I couldn't make the first class, but I just want to make a little one, for a bird," she tells him rather sheepishly. He says that's okay, but she detects a note of disappointment in his voice.

Jacque is a good teacher, patient and he explains things clearly, and helps Sarah with the tricky parts, because this is the only class she can attend. During their break, one of the other students tells her that Jacque makes birch bark canoes in the traditional manner, and he's been written about in the newspapers; that he's kind of famous around Grand Marais. And that in addition to the Make Your Own Coffin class, he teaches a Make Your Own Snowshoe workshop each January. A short elderly woman says she takes a class Wednesday nights from his cousin, and that they're making Cree lubbuks. Her husband shows them a big sliver in his thumb and then pours everyone a half a paper cup of coffee from a big plaid thermos, and then they all go back to work.

At the end of class Jacque says he hopes she can come back next fall and make her own, and she can tell he really hopes she will come back. He's nice. Maybe she will. Maybe she and Morgan can come up and make their own coffins. Why not? On the way home the lake is a dark smoky blue, and a ribbon of orange floats low across the sky, and Glancing down at the little box on the seat beside her she feels a sense of accomplishment much larger than carpentry.

---

SARAH CAN HARDLY BELIEVE it's her last night. She feels at home sitting in front of the fire with a cup of tea, just watching the flames. It's easy to start a fire with birch bark and logs now, and she loves the aroma. She's been thinking of calling Stephen. Just a quick call to say hello, to see how he's doing. But she probably doesn't have his number. Checking her address book, she's surprised to find she has the number. She stands beside the picture window, looking out at the yard past the clothes line to where she usually sees the deer, gathering up courage, or whatever she seems to need from the night outside, before she calls.

"Stephen?"

"Sarah? What a surprise. How are you? Is everything okay?"

"Well, yes. I just thought I'd call. I'm at a friend's house up by Grand Marais. About 40 miles from Canada. I'm by myself on a retreat. I've been here for a week."

"By yourself? What kind of retreat? Yoga, I would guess. Are you okay, a week by yourself?"

"I'm fine. It's just a retreat – kind of a general retreat. I do yoga in the mornings, and take walks. I sit and look at the lake."

"I see,"

"Do you ever hear things, Stephen? I mean like voices?"

The silence on Stephen's end of the phone lasts so long that Sarah thinks they may have been disconnected.

"Are you there? Stephen?'

"Yes. Sure, I'm here. Why do you ask – about voices, I mean."

"Well, I was just wondering. I think its okay, you know, if you hear things, sort of unusual things, sometimes," Sarah says.

"I agree completely. And if some people don't hear voices, things, that's okay too," he says.

"Life is mysterious, isn't it?" she says.

"Especially in Minnesota," Stephen replies, quite surprising Sarah. Then he laughs, that laugh she so loves.

"Oh Stephen, now I know you're okay. Guess I just wanted to hear your voice. I'm going to hang up now. Morgan picks me up tomorrow."

"Wait. Sarah, did you meet Laura?

"Yes. I like her."

"Me too," Stephen sighs. "She keeps me normal. But Sarah, if you ever need to talk, about voices or wolves or anything. Just call me."

"Thanks, Stephen. And you take care of yourself too. Night then."

"Night, Sarah."

She opens a bottle of ale and sits beside the fire until the bottle is empty. By the time she has put on her gown and robe and closed the drapes, a line for a poem has begun to form. The last few evenings she has ended the day by writing a poem while sitting by the fire's final embers. She is working on the poem she started last night, after a visit to a rocky part of the shore where she thinks she saw an otter. It was a small dark-headed animal swimming around a rocky ridge and she liked the soft paddling sounds it made as it swam out of sight. Morgan would have known right away whether it was an otter or something else. For the poem, she declares it an otter.

*You saw some herring bones*
*and I found a comb*
*back inside the otter's cave*
*that day beside the shore.*

*We sat and let our feet float out*
*and bob there by the rocks;*
*the wind inside the waves*
*forgot to leave our hearts alone.*

She sighs, wondering who she's writing about, then burns the poem in the last of the embers. "We sat and let our feet float out," she recites the line now turned to smoke. Whose feet? Hers and Morgan's? Stephen's? Jacque, the coffin maker's, or some ghostly companion? Or maybe not a person at all, but some general kind of floating pleasantness that includes everyone, everything.

———————

HER FINAL MORNING ARRIVES. Everything is packed, and she has an hour or so before Morgan is due. She wants to finish before he arrives, and hurries to the ravine with the shovel and the hand-made coffin. She hadn't seen exactly where Lowell tossed the bird so she searches along the ravine for some time before she finds it, half hidden in the tall grass. The death smell is slight, thanks to the cool fall weather. Her heart beats unreasonably loud and fast when she peers down close, surprised at finding it at all, thinking it might have been just another figment of her imagination. And it was surprising it hadn't been carried off by a coyote or a fox, or one of the timber wolves Jacque said were so abundant up by The Holy Land. She shudders as she plucks a neck feather and tucks it into her pocket. She takes just one photograph of the bird, then digs a reasonably deep hole, sets down the coffin and uses the shovel to place the bird into the box. She finishes up and says a prayer. A big truck carrying logs drives by as she heads back to the house.

She is sitting on the porch with her feet propped on the moose antler when Morgan drives in.

"Hello, hello," Morgan says, getting out of the car and rushing over to Sarah. "How was it? How are you? So good to see you." Morgan holds Sarah in his arms for a long time, until another truck carrying logs drives past, raising the dust.

------------

AT THEIR PARK POINT HOUSE, Sarah finds that she needs to touch the walls as she walks through the rooms. She touches the woodwork and the windows, runs her hand along the backs of chairs, along the wood and stone countertops, the books and CDs, and along the black sheen of the piano. She slips off her socks so she can feel the smooth wooden boards of the flooring, the cool tile in the kitchen. She presses her toes into the Persian carpet in the big room as if reading the rug's pattern and texture in some form of foot Braille. Upstairs, Morgan's workroom is cluttered with paper, books, glasses, and cups of half-finished tea.

The teapot whistles loudly from downstairs in the kitchen. Now what kind of tea would he be brewing? He keeps surprising her lately. She was surprised when they left Grand Marais and then ten miles down the road he turned in at the Lake Superior Lodge. She had always wanted to stay at the resort but had never mentioned that to Morgan, who had spent many weeks at the resort as a child, on vacation with his parents. The main lodge had great carved wooden beams, a huge stone fireplace and a spectacular view of Lake Superior. She and Morgan had dinner in the lodge and then swam in the adjoining pool. While soaking in the hot tub they both let old cares melt away and by the time they got back to their cabin, they were like young lovers on a honeymoon.

In the late evening they had walked to the beach to see Mars over the lake. Morgan said it was closer to the earth than it would ever be again in their lifetimes. Sarah saw it right away across the lake, reddish and so bright it cast its light across the lake as if it were the moon. They stood watching Mars and the stars while the water sloshed rhythmically in and out from shore a few steps from their feet.

To Sarah, Morgan's workroom is like a large school room or a laboratory. Two of the walls hold nothing but books and maps. There is a large blackboard, a conglomeration of computer equipment, several globes and telescopes, and a cheerful painting of parrots. The center piece of the room is a twenty-foot custom-made work table. Sarah peruses the papers on the table top. Most seem to be about light refraction, with diagrams and Morgan's signature convoluted calculations,, which also cover the blackboard. There are old clippings about lighthouses and stacks of books. She picks up a yellowed newspaper article with a picture of Split Rock Lighthouse and smiles to herself. She feels good today, renewed.

They have Jasmine tea on the deck, even though it is quite cool. Next spring Morgan plans to have the lower deck made into a year-round room. The tower will be built at the same time.

Sarah goes through her mail as she sips tea. She first opens the registration confirmation for a sculpture class she signed up for at UMD. Now that Morgan has taken a position at UMD, they can ride to school together when her classes begin. She slides a round card of a moon out of a square envelope. It's an invitation to an engagement party for Lulu and Leif, at Lilly's house this Saturday afternoon. Everyone is asked to bring a song to sing or a poem to read or some surprise entertainment to share. Lulu's handwritten PS reads "Devi is in Duluth!" She hands the invitation to Morgan.

# *four*

---

MORGAN AND SARAH SIT WAITING for a boat. They have recently started checking the Shipping News arrivals and departures, but this is the end of the season. The boat leaving the harbor is loaded with wheat, "Milo, a Greek ship, built in 1984," Morgan says, recalling the details from the Shipping News. This week ships have come in to pick up taconite, coal, and wheat. The unusual item was flax. Sarah recalls seeing fields of flax in bloom near Canada, fields of blue flowers as blue as a lake. Morgan too, has seen the flax fields in bloom. Coming home from boarding school as a young man, he was fascinated by the strange blue squares of flax he saw from the plane, like square lakes of blue.

"Lilly has a patch of flax in her back yard, I had almost forgotten," Sarah muses as the bridge lowers to street level.

Driving over the bridge, Sarah adjusts the bows on the presents for Lulu and Leif, two small Henning carvings from Norway, one of a woman in a bright red folk costume and the other of a fisherman in a yellow slicker. She hopes they like them. She and Morgan each picked one out from Berquist Scandinavian Imports up in Cloquet.

The boat held them up longer than usual, and they are the last to arrive at Lilly's.

"Morgan, will you fix this doorbell for Lilly?"

"I'll take a look before we leave."

202

They let themselves in and find everyone in Lilly's bedroom huddled around a screen, watching Sam Light speaking to them from his jail cell. He is telling how the second edition of his book on mushrooms has been doing well and he bought his computer equipment with the royalties. Now he's working on a book called "A Life of Crime in Black and White."

"Good title," Stephen says, staring at Sam sitting in the visitor's computer room of his jail. What might have been, what might have been, he sighs. Still, he's glad Lilly invited him, even though it had been last minute, when he and Laura were buying fruit at the Kenwood SuperOne and Lilly was there with her son from India, buying supplies for the party. From the computer, a guard's voice shouts out "time's up." Sam says he has to go, that it's dinner time there. The huddle around the computer breaks up as the screen goes black and Lilly shuts down the computer.

On his way to the kitchen Stephen can hear Lilly telling Devi to buy this equipment so they can talk and visit like that when he goes back to Delhi. Lulu hands Stephen a plate of lefse which she and Lilly made last night. They heard about using Nutella from Jeep who said they use it in Paris, on their crepes. It's chocolate and hazel nuts ground to a smooth paste. "It's good!" Lulu says.

Stephen carries the curious tray of lefse to the table set up on the deck and he compliments Lulu on her Norwegian folk costume. It's funny, he had been thinking about writing a book on crime – on his crime. Certainly no life of crime in black and white. His was more just an episode, or an incident. Was it black and white? Is it ever? Now when he thinks about it, it feels more like high definition color.

Just a week ago when he was trying to sleep he was thinking about how much more interesting a book on his crime would be than the book on icons he's doing for the University Press. He had even considered titles, and he remembers falling asleep while wavering between "A Man Possessed," and "What the eyes made me do." And that was the last night he heard James Cagney, who told him "Just go to sleep. Let it go." Now he seems to be gone. So far. What a beautiful Indian summer afternoon it is. Why is it that he is here, a free man, and Sam Light is sitting in jail? Stephen shakes his head at the wonder of it.

"Hey, Stephen, how are you?" Gigi comes up beside him.

"Gigi. I was thinking about jail. Glad I'm here and not there. Actually, I'm pretty good. I go to church. Just sit there. No conversion or anything. I just like to sit there." Laura joins them and Stephen puts his arm around her. "Have you two met?" They both laugh, which puzzles Stephen, but he smiles as they walk out toward the yard.

Sarah and Devi carry copper chai glasses out to the deck and Devi gets his sitar out of its case. Sarah stands at the railing, surprised to see Morgan and Gigi looking at the cherry bushes by the side of the garage.

"Hey, Sarah," Jeep says, coming up beside her and looking down toward Gigi and Morgan. "That's trouble waiting to happen."

"Oh Jeep, hello. Nice to see you. We met when I came home from the hospital but I was not very alert that day," Sarah says, offering her hand. She is surprised to find him so homely and yet at the same time attractive, in that manner of confident men.

"Gigi's asking him stuff. Making him feel smart," Jeep says. "That's her technique."

"You can't control Gigi, or anyone – what they're going to do, they'll do," Sarah says. "I have a sort of dumb trust lately. I hope for the best."

"I trust too. For the worst. People do what they can get away with," Jeep says.

"I think they can tell," Sarah says. "I mean what we're thinking. If you know someone believes in you, loves you, they'll act differently."

Jeep laughs, a dark laugh, but with just enough hopefulness to make Sarah like him somewhat.

"Let's not leave it to luck," Jeep says. "Hey Gigi," he calls out loudly.

Gigi waves and walks toward the deck ahead of Morgan, walking like a beautiful woman who knows she is being watched. She walks slowly, like an elegant cat. She could be balancing a basket of papayas on her head. Even Devi watches Gigi walk. Like a woman in a Fellini movie, Sarah later tells Morgan.

From inside the house, Leif's laugh ricochets like BBs.

*His laughter, like monkeys set free.*

---

THE FORMAL PROCESSION BEGINS: Leif and Lulu come to the deck arm in arm, Lulu in the antique Norwegian folk costume she inherited from her grandmother and Leif in Lederhosen, a white shirt with bow tie, a dark green jacket much too large for his slim frame, and a French beret. Lulu wears a wreath of white flowers in her bluish white hair. The engaged couple are both proud and happy.

Lilly follows them out, wearing a rose-colored sari and shawl and carrying a bouquet of wild roses. Tom Troll and Devi follow, Tom in a flannel shirt and tie, his hands folded formally in front of him. He walks slowly like a priest. Devi looks like visiting royalty in a deep red sherwani, his dark eyes sparkling with good health and joy. Julia, the actress, seems to float across the deck, a Chagall figure come to life in a long blue silk dress, carrying a bouquet of brightly colored maple branches, arm in arm with her handsome young boyfriend, the runner from Sweden.

Stephen and Laura walk slowly and formally along, and Gigi, in a diaphanous peach gown, does her famous walk across the deck and down the stairs to join the procession on the lawn. She is followed closely by Jeep, who takes her hand at the bottom of the stairs.

Leif's sister-in-law, Ethel, is dressed in black and wears a small hat that resembles a former crow. She smiles at everyone and joins the group. Lulu's sister, Lena, takes a few careful steps using her cane, then settles into her wheel chair at the side of the deck.

Morgan and Sarah are the last in the parade, as Sarah was chilly and went back inside to borrow one of Lilly's shawls. Morgan looks at Sarah wearing Lilly's lavender afghan over her shoulders as if he has never seen anything so wonderful as she. Sarah actually blushes as they join the procession.

Leif hadn't wanted music until after they ate, so the only music of the procession around the yard is the sound of a few birds singing high in the trees, and the crunching of crisp fall leaves beneath everyone's feet. Yellow leaves from the old birch fall as they walk, drifting down like butterflies.

Lulu and Leif complete the walk around the backyard and stop before the small table covered with a white table cloth, set with flowers, two candle sticks and a large sheet cake. This is when Leif had wanted to do a ten round salute, but Lilly talked him into lighting candles instead. Leif takes off his beret and holds his hand over his heart for a moment before he lights the candles, which sizzle and sparkle, delighting Leif and Lulu like children at a birthday party.

After the candles are lit, Morgan and Jeep open the champagne and Lilly pours chai. The cake is cut and the food is readied, while Devi's sitar music drifts over the celebration. The table is laid with chutneys and pickles, cranberry sauce, smoked wild Alaskan Salmon, wild rice, jasmine rice, red dal, veggie samosas, rutabaga puffs, sauerkraut, and a silver pot of potato leek soup and another of black bean and sweet potato stew. There are cherry tomatoes and cheese – Jarlsberg, Swiss, Brie, and fresh Gjetost; homemade Swedish limpa bread, rye flat breads, naan bread, lefse, rommegrot with raspberry sauce, blueberry pie, raspberry-rhubarb pie, and home-made black current ice cream.

By the time the champagne, chai, and food have been consumed, the afternoon has cooled considerably and everyone settles into lawn chairs in the backyard. Julie and Gigi pass out wool Hudson Bay blankets, one to each person. Jeep says it's like being on the deck of the Queen Mary in the olden days. Stephen hopes it's not the *Titanic* and he thinks of the little man he met who lost his brother when the Edmund Fitzgerald went down.

"What are you mumbling about, Stephen," Gigi asks.

"Oh nothing. Just hoping for the best.'"

"Me too," Gigi says and asks what he is doing for the program, but instead of waiting for his answer she tells him about the dance she has been working on for a week.

Finally everyone is settled, and Jeep and Lilly act as emcees and announce the acts. First is Julia, with the Oh Holy Night recipe song, requested by Leif. Julia's Swedish boyfriend accompanies on guitar, and the refrains of Oh Holy Night fill the air on the fine autumn day in Duluth with the words to a hot dish recipe. "One o-n-ion..." Again, Leif cries, and Julia's voice, with the guitar accompaniment, is as pure and beautiful as the blue of the sky above the yard.

Everyone has an offering, of sorts. Some are predictable, some not. Stephen reads a poem by Alfred Lord Tennyson, and Laura reads a poem of her own composition about the beauty of fall leaves. Sarah follows, reading Robert Frost's "The Road Not Taken."

Gigi performs her dance, using scarves, with accompaniment by Devi on sitar. She prances around the backyard, tossing her head to and fro, stopping to listen to something in the sky – turning her head this way and that and opening her eyes wide as if in disbelief. Gigi is graceful and beautiful, though her timing is peculiar and her sense of drama exaggerated. Everyone applauds when she finishes, led by Jeep, who calls out "Bravo, Bravo." Gigi takes a formal operatic bow.

Jeep's offering is a reading of the First Amendment to the Constitution, which is eloquent, even if not quite fitting of the occasion, except to Jeep.

Morgan takes his place on the deck, which is also the stage, carrying a drum. He sits down and plays the drum and half sings and half recites a marriage song from an Amazon region of Brazil. It is much like a chant and Lilly spontaneously adds vocal accompaniment and Julia joins in to harmonize. Morgan gets a round of applause, quite surprising and pleasing to him.

Tom plays a song on the penny whistle, surprising everyone, including himself. Later, he explains how he knows only the one song, but he thinks now he may look into taking lessons, if he can find a teacher.

To end the program, Lena and Ethel take turns reading from the Bible. Lena reads the first half of the Twenty-third Psalm and Ethel reads the ending. Jeep steps around the house as soon as they begin so no one will see his reaction. Stephen shakes his head, "Who is he to criticize, reading the First Amendment," he comments to Laura, who smiles understandingly.

The audience applauds politely for the Twenty-third Psalm, and they finish the celebration with freshly brewed Peace coffee served on Sarah's mother's best china. Leif plays the accordion and everyone sets aside their blankets and rises to the occasion to polka and waltz in the backyard of falling leaves. Finally, worn out and happy, the guests depart with the news that Leif and Lulu will be married in Las Vegas next weekend in the Elvis Chapel.

*part 4*

WINTER

# *one*

A LAYER OF NEW SNOW COVERS the city of Duluth and the houses on the hillside spout puffs of smoke from their chimney tops. The sky is a dazzling azure above the white rolling hills and the frozen blue lake spreads outward like a fuzzy wool baby's blanket. On the ski trail behind St. Scholastica, the only sound is the scrunch of Morgan and Sarah's skis as they cross a snowy slope on the old Stations of the Cross trail.

This is it," Sarah says. "The burnt house. Actually I never saw the house. It's always been like this. Just the fireplace and these cement edges over there."

They take off their gear and light the new Sterno stove. The beans heat quickly and Sarah fills their paper plates and adds the cheese and Christmas bread Lilly insisted they take along. Morgan pours coffee from the thermos. "You have rosy cheeks," he says between bites.

"So do you. I think we're starting to feel at home here." Morgan smiles and sips his coffee. "Funny, how long it's taken, considering that we both grew up in Duluth." They both know he means they're feeling at home together.

Sarah sighs. She tells Morgan about skiing here with Gigi and her old friend Jen, back when they were all in high school. They had a picnic right here. Had beans then too. And a little gin, from Gigi's brother. She had it in a flask. We called ourselves Mrs. Leland's Ski Club. She shakes her head, not knowing how they came up with the name. She didn't know any Mrs. Leland but one of them must have. They had wanted to make some money so they made up the club so they could sell the World's Finest candy bars. They still sell that brand. She always buys them, whenever anyone's kids are selling them, for whatever reason. They're much smaller now days, but still pretty good chocolate bars.

You needed to have a club with officers in order to sell the candy and so Gigi was the president, Sarah was secretary and Jen was treasurer. They each had an entire cardboard box full of candy bars to sell. "My dad bought a lot of my candy bars," she tells Morgan. And Gigi's family bought half of hers. Jen's little brother ate most of hers and she had to baby sit to pay for them.

They had what seemed like a huge bill to pay, which they did, in the end, but they didn't make a cent from their venture. "Jen kept babysitting to pay her share, and Gigi and I ended up selling the last of our boxes down on Park Point when the smelt were running and we went from fire to fire along the beach selling our candy. Sarah can still see the silvery smelt in pails beside the fires, and the fish roasting in aluminum foil. "I never liked eating smelt. I felt sorry for them." She says.

"I remember when they had a Smelt Queen," Morgan laughs.

"Then they couldn't get anyone to run."

"I never did try smelting," Morgan says.

Sarah went every year. She used to rescue the smelt. Take them out of the nets and throw them back in the water when no one was looking, especially the big ones. They'd fish on the sand bars. You could walk way out into the lake along the sand if you knew where to go and the water would only come up to your thighs. She went out with the nets a few times. You had to wear hip boots and there was a kind of suction of water against the rubber boots and you could feel the heaviness of the water against your legs and it was like feeling the weight of the whole lake around you, yet you could still walk. The nets were long, maybe 80 feet long. In any case long enough that now she couldn't remember who was on the other end. Her brother David probably, or her dad.

They would start at the shore and walk out slowly, holding the pole end of the net parallel to the water just above the surface until you were about a half a block out into the lake. Then you would lower the net so the pole just touched the bottom. Next you would start walking slowly toward shore while keeping the pole just skimming the bottom. You had to watch the water and not the fires along the shore, otherwise you might trip. Walking through the water like that, in the dark, was like walking in a dream, or in some other time or place.

"I loved it, Morgan. I think there was moonlight, but it was the sound of walking through water that I loved. A really soft sound. And when you finally got to shore you would raise your end of the net at the same time as your partner and then everyone would come with flashlights to see what you caught. Sometimes the net was really heavy and full of fish and other times it seemed heavy but there would be just a few smelt jumping in the middle of the net. And all those fires along the beach for as far as you could see. That was something. Funny, thinking about that here in the snow. Same place though. Right here with our beans. Gigi wasn't much of a skier."

Morgan is enjoying Sarah's stories. How wound up and happy she seems. He had to go far away to see fishing like that, he tells her. They sit quietly for a while, finishing their coffee, both thinking about fishing and how little they've known of one another.

"Your turn," she says. "Tell me something I don't know."

He tells how he never skied up here before and that he learned to ski in Switzerland. His mother loved the Alps and his dad liked Zurich, the city of business. They would stay in Zurich and then Grindelwald because it was nearby. But he skied more in Aspen. That's where he really became interested in preserving the land and the mountains. He used to look for mountain goats. He thinks Aspen is where he grew up and became a more serious person, he tells her. "So here we are!" Morgan says, slapping his gloves together.

Packing up and getting into their skis, Sarah realizes she's just getting to know her husband. Why have they never talked like this until this year?

They ski on past the maple grove and stop at the top of a cliff overlooking a vast valley and the city and lake beyond.

"I think I see our house," Sarah says. "Two or three houses past that red building. The school. Isn't that our house?"

"I would need binoculars. I can't see that far."

"I think that's it. We should get a pair of those light binoculars and just keep them in the car," she says, then pushes off and glides down the hill, rounding the corner with precision and grace. She waits for Morgan where the trail levels off, at the empty shrine, a ten-foot tall stone structure with a niche for a statue, which is missing.

Morgan stops beside Sarah with a quick turn. "I had my picture taken here once. I sat where the missing statue would have been. I must have seen the statue once, really long ago, but mostly it's been empty like this." The stone shrine is monumental in its wooded setting in the snow, leaving what the statue was like to their imaginations.

"Ready?" Morgan asks. This time Morgan takes off first, telemarking down the steepest hill of the trail. When Sarah catches up they ski together to Kenwood Avenue, where they take off their skis to cross the road to the end of the Chester Park trail. On the other side, as soon as they are a block along the trail, a deer crosses in front of them, kicking up its heels in the soft snow. They watch the deer bound off through the trees before skiing on to the hill above the ski jumps. They stop to watch the jumpers, and Sarah spots Leif down below standing near the skiing side of the frozen lake, leaning on a shovel.

"I am really starting to feel at home," Morgan says. "Let's go home and make a fire. We can pick up a pizza from Pizza Luce."

"Sounds good. Let's have some music too. Maybe Norah Jones, or some old jazz," she says.

"Okay. Maybe we'll dance," Morgan says playfully, as he pushes off down the ski trail toward their car. They race to the parking lot. By the time the skis are fastened to the top of the car the sun is beginning to set, and as they drive along Skyline Parkway the sky is red above the lake and the ice and snow of Duluth are beginning to glow as if lit by a fire from within.

# Acknowledgements

Thank you to my good friends and relatives for your encouragement, enthusiasm, and advice. And thank you to Kathy and Lowell for your generosity in loaning me the use of your fabulous house "Up North," a place that inspires the most creative of dreams. Thanks to all of my early readers, especially Erik, and to Mary, and Shirley, for their helpful final edits.

Thanks to Lane for his cover photo of the ski jump at Chester Bowl, taken the month before it was dismantled by the city. May it always be remembered.

And most of all, thank you to my mother, who raised me to appreciate my Norwegian heritage, including all the trolls and gnomes of the world.

www.ingramcontent.com/pod-product-compliance
Lightning Source LLC
Chambersburg PA
CBHW032049240626
47154CB00003B/1141